ARE YOU
KIDDIN'
ME?

ARE YOU KIDDIN' ME?

A medley of humorous short stories

Anirban Das

Srishti
PUBLISHERS & DISTRIBUTORS

SRISHTI PUBLISHERS & DISTRIBUTORS
Registered Office: N-16, C.R. Park
New Delhi – 110 019
Corporate Office: 212A, Peacock Lane
Shahpur Jat, New Delhi – 110 049
editorial@srishtipublishers.com

First published by
Srishti Publishers & Distributors in 2019

Declaration: The stories are works of fiction and fantasy. Similarity of any character/s with any personality, living, dead or in transit, is unintentional and completely coincidental.

The author asserts the moral right to be identified as the author of this work.

Dear reader,

Thank you for selecting this book. Trust you will have as much fun reading this book as I had while writing it.

Once you are done, could I request you to share your feedback on Amazon and Goodreads?

Till then, happy reading ☺

Cheers,
Anirban

PS: Best enjoyed with a steaming hot cup of tea or coffee, and sizzling onion pakodas.

Contents

Bossy affair

The perils of taking impulsive decisions when a frustrated   66
employee stuck with a tyrannical boss decides to switch jobs.

Turbulence

Contrasts the varying emotions and actions of a frequent flyer   108
(suave urbanite) with a first time flyer (country yokel) when they
experience a mid-air crisis.

The pitch

Reiterates the adage that there is no such thing as free lunch,   122
dinner (or even tea and samosa, for that matter).

Expectations

Highlights the expectation and resulting disappointment   135
(two sides of the same coin) of a bank employee when his son
apparently goofs up in his exams.

Faceoff

Presents a what-if situation in which a man has an out of body   147
experience and grapples with an identity crisis, but ends up
getting a whole new perspective on life.

Snorefest

The problem of snoring and the devastation caused by it on   160
innocent bystanders.

Memory bytes

Projects a fantastic possibility, wherein a student gets a magical   170
power, but also pays the price.

Gubbara Yadav's adventure

A disgruntled bull realizes that while the grass may be greener   192
on the other side, home is where the heart is.

The Venture Capitalist

'Smoking Kills'

Seated on a cramped wooden chair at a small tea joint, I kept staring listlessly at the terse warning at the bottom of the cigarette packet. A man with multi coloured lungs was looking up at me from the packet, pointing a finger at me accusingly. Nonchalantly, I swung my forearm and deftly placed the forefinger and middle finger of my right hand onto my lips. Sucking on the filter of a freshly lit cigarette, I closed my eyes and inhaled deeply. I may have lacked a few qualities, but style was not one of them.

"*Aahhh…cough… cough… cough.*"

The sound caught the attention of a beautiful young girl, seated a few paces away from me. She was dressed in casual jeans and a white t-shirt. She held a book in her right hand and a cutting chai in her left. For a fleeting moment, I forgot to cough and flashed a smile at the girl with the hope of reciprocity. The girl looked at me disdainfully and got back to reading her book. I had the disturbing feeling that she might have shown me the finger too, but this could not be confirmed.

I was not going to give up so easily, *no sir*. I tried again (with the cigarette[1], not the girl), this time with a shallow intake. Puckering my lips like a jellyfish, I tried to exhale the remnants into discrete nebulous smoke rings.

'*Hoooooooooooooooooo*'.

All that emanated from my mouth was a thick gush of chimney smoke.

Damn*%$#@**!

Maybe I should have transitioned to bidis. Cigging was a recent cultivation, an indirect consequence of my futile efforts in scouting funding for my grandiose new business idea: Book Summaries. It was a multi-billion dollar (give or take a few zeros) idea which would disrupt the book reading business. *An exclusive summary for every book; how cool was that?* Applying the brilliance of my MBA brain, the total value creation would be five hours of productive reading time compressed to five minutes x the number of books read every day x reading population=???

Well, a whole lot of hours saved every year, anyway!

I was sure that I had a winner until I started reaching out to friends and relatives. Magically, most of them seemed to be unreachable or had simply disappeared. The silver lining was that almost everyone had ample stock of expert advice, waiting to be unleashed. I provided the trigger.

I decided to up the ante, by knocking on the doors of angel investors[2] and vulture[3] capitalists. Knocking gave way rapidly to banging, and thereafter to pleading and begging. 'No' was not in my lexicon, as I was able to eke out access to a few individuals

---

[1] Romanticism associated with cigarette smoking is a myth.

[2] Angel investor is a misnomer; there is nothing remotely 'angelic' about this breed.

[3] This is NOT a typo.

by wearing down their patience and evoking their sympathy. The outcome was predictably boring in all the meetings. What troubled me was not so much the outcome, but the IQ levels of these individuals, as could be judged by the level of their inane questions. Sample these:

"If your idea is so good, why do you think there is not a single big name in this space?"

< Silence > *(That's because this is a creative, unique, brilliant idea. And I am a genius even if I am not saying it out loud).*

"Do you have partners?"

< Silence > *(Are you crazy? Why the hell would I want to share my control and profits with others?)*

"You know, we are looking for passion in an entrepreneur."

< Silence > *(I have passion in kilos, my middle name is passion).*

"Do you have a working proto business model? How can you prove that you have a scalable model?"

< Silence > < Silence >.

"How are you going to address copyright issues? Will you not face opposition from the authors?"

< Silence > < Silence >.< Silence >.

"How much skin do you have in the game?"

<Very long Silence >.

Wading through my smoke screen in the tea joint, I couldn't help ruing the fact that there were so many obstacles for fresh new ideas and talent in this country.

"Sir, *joota polish?*" a voice spoke up, out of nowhere.

My reverie had been broken. I looked up to locate the source, but saw no one.

"Sir, *joota polish?*" the voice repeated itself in a distinct childlike strain.

I looked down this time; it was a small boy no taller than a cricket bat, around seven years old. The boy wore a tattered t-shirt on the inside and covered it up with an oversized crumpled shirt, which reached his knees. Sporting an impish smile accentuated by his untidy, coarse tufts of hair splayed carelessly in myriad directions, and a set of perfectly white teeth, the boy repeated his question.

"Sir, *joota polish? Aapke joote ekdum chamka denge, woh naye jaise lagenge aur bilkul aap film ke hero jaise, sir,*"said the boy, waving a shoe brush close to my face.

My eyes caught a glimpse of the boy's feet and noticed that he was bare feet. He was looking at me expectantly with large eager eyes. I then looked down at my shoes and it dawned on me as to how dirty they were. A shiner was surely due, but employing the services of this boy was out of the question. I pretended to check some calls on my mobile phone.

Observing my reticence, the boy collapsed the fingers of his right hand, clutching onto an imaginary morsel of food and shoving it into his mouth repeatedly. He followed this up with a quick rub of his non-existent belly.

"Sir, no *khaana pura din.*One chance, please. Not happy, then *paisa waapas. Roti ki kasam.*"The increased usage of English language in the boy's pleas did not go unnoticed, as he waited for me to take the bait. I relented a little.

"*Naam kya hai tumhara?*"

"Iqbal, sir."

"Hmmmmm," I replied with a great deal of gravity, wondering what to say next.

"Sir, *aapka naam?*" Iqbal asked out the blue, taking me by surprise.

"Ambareesh."

"Amrish."

"*Nahi, nahi.*Ambareesh."

"Amrish," the boy repeated.

"*No, Am-baa-reesh.*" I said in an agitated tone. *Name mispronunciations, I couldn't stand. Especially mine.*

"Amrish," the boy repeated yet again.

I threw my hands up and sighed. "Yes, Amrish."

The boy smiled benignly and extended his right hand towards me. I was pleasantly surprised by the kid's confidence and reciprocated by extending my hand towards his to complete the handshake.

Iqbal shot a puzzled expression towards me and withdrew his hand, pointing towards my shoes this time. "Sir, *joote nikalenge* please," he requested politely.

Embarrassed, I meekly removed my dusty shoes and handed them over to Iqbal. The big toe of my right foot stood out from the gaping hole in the sock. I hurriedly slipped my right foot below my left.

I watched Iqbal intently, as he applied a few brush strokes on my shoes to try and reduce the thickness of the dust layers. Thereafter, he whipped out a tin of mouldy, partially dried out cake of shoe polish from his shirt pocket, dabbed the brush in the tin hurriedly and applied the goo onto my shoes. Iqbal then scrubbed the shoes vigorously with the brush in his little hands. After two minutes of intense scrubbing, Iqbal proudly held up the shoes for display.

"*Badiya shine na*, sir?" asked Iqbal, looking at me expectantly with his toothy smile.

I had to admit that the original black colour was visible again, though in varying hues, little thanks to the generous splotches of the polish. It was not a perfect job, but I could now pay off the kid quickly and lighten my conscience. I removed my wallet and perused its contents. There was a single five hundred rupee note and some change.

Before I could extract anything, Iqbal spoke up. "Sir, *ek 500 rupaiah ka note milega?*"

I was aghast, not believing what I had heard. Sympathy went out of the window. I bawled, "500 bucks for a polish? That's looting!" (In times of distress, I could mouth only English words).

Iqbal seemed to interpret what I was ranting as he tried to reassure me by waving his little palms in opposite directions. "*Na, na sir. Shoe polish free, aapse money no. Mujhe ek shoe kit kharidna hai, lekin paisa nahin. Roti ki kasam... Aap thoda help karoge?*"

I looked at Iqbal with suspicion.

"*Sir, main bahut mehnat karoonga. Main shoe polish karke school jaana chahta hoon. Main aapka paisa pie pie waapas kar doonga. Roti ki kasam.*"

There was something very earnest about Iqbal's appeal. He was offering me a chance to be a 'good' person. *Hell, I could be his benefactor, his very own venture capitalist! Now that was an idea.*

I could lend Iqbal 500 bucks and ask him to return 600. Surely he would not have a problem with that. I did a mental math calculation. One shoe shine boy, profit margin – 100 bucks. One million shoe shine boys in the city, profit margin – 100 million bucks![4] Today: shoe shine boys. Tomorrow: shoe-shine parlours. Day after tomorrow: Online shoe service (*whatever that meant*). This made so much more sense than the book summary idea, which was not going anywhere anyway.

I could already visualise my name in *Forbes* and *Time* magazines.

'Visionary venture capitalist becomes king of shoe polishing trade.'(*No, that didn't sound right.*)

'Bill Gates says Ambareesh is an inspiration in both business & philanthropy.'

'Ambareesh wins the Nobel peace prize.'

Iqbal brought me out of my trance by waving his brush next to my face again. "*Sir, sir, aap kahan ho? Aap mera help karoge na?*"

---

[4]   Source of figures – Thin air.

I gave an intense look at Iqbal and decided that I had some serious questioning to do.

"*Pehle kuch* answers *do.*"

"*Kaise answers*, sir?"

"Tell me, *is* business *mein tumhara* partner *kaun bangega?*"

Iqbal scratched his head and shot me a confused look. "Sir, *nahin samjha.*"

"*Accha* leave it. *Yeh batao*, game *mein* skin *kitna hai?*"

Iqbal stood perplexed. "*Kisme kya hai?*"

"Never mind. *Yeh batao, tumhare idea mein kya khaas hai?* Competition *ko kaise* handle *karoge?*"

There was a long silence after which Iqbal shot me a dirty look this time. "Sir, *paisa dena hai to do, nahi to mat do. Time paas mat karo.*"

Aha, the boy had pride! For reasons unexplained, I saw glimpses of myself in Iqbal and felt a connection. Basic instinct told me this boy would fulfil his promise. Basic instinct: the core competency of venture capitalists. I was mighty pleased with myself, having discovered a new talent at such a young age. *(I am talking about myself, not Iqbal.)*

"Sir, sir, sir?" Iqbal interrupted my thought process.

"*Aah*, yes, yes." I took out a 500 rupee note and held it forth. "Okay Iqbal, I believe you. I am going to invest in you and mentor you personally. I am going to make you a star in the shoe shine business. Go forth and make me proud, my boy."

Iqbal snatched the note from my hand and smiled at me sweetly. "Sir, *kya bola kuch bhi samajh mein nahin aaya. Main aaj hi kit khareedoonga aur mehnat karke aapka saara paise agle hafte hi lauta doonga. Roti ki kasam.*"

I smiled back. "*Bahut tez bacchhe ho. Bahut aage jaaoge. Lekin agle hafte, 500 nahin, 600 rupaiah wapas karna. 100 rupaiah mera profit. Theek hai?*"

"Yes, sir. *Aap mere liye bhagwan hai.*"

I beamed smugly, but said modestly, "*Nahi, main sirf ek venture capitalist hoon jo tumhari madat karna chahta hai. Kuch aur dosto ko aisi madad chahiye toh bolna.*"

Iqbal bent down to touch my feet. I could see that he was struggling hard to fight back his tears. I also felt like crying, but held myself back. It was then that I noticed the waiter who had been standing close by. He looked at me and nodded his head in approval. The tea joint owner standing behind the cash counter, seemed to be rotating his head left and right. I couldn't figure out if he had a pain in his neck or if he was trying to tell me something.

Iqbal left the joint with a promise (*of the roti*) to meet me next Monday, along with a few of his friends. I couldn't wait to meet Iqbal and his friends.

Monday came after a long time. Iqbal was running late. I checked my watch repeatedly, but there was no sign of him or his friends. Maybe I had misheard Iqbal. I came back again on Tuesday and waited. But Iqbal was nowhere to be seen. I made appearances in the tea joint each day thereafter, for the next one week, but Iqbal seemed to have vanished from the face of the earth.

Finally one day, the tea joint owner walked up to me. "Do not waste your time, sir. That boy was no shoe shine boy; he was a part of a nomadic group. That group has long moved away to another location."

I was stunned. I fidgeted with my cutting chai and stared at the tea joint owner. His words kept replaying in my mind. Finally I said, "*Kya bola, kuch samajh mein nahin aaya. Roti ki kasam.*"

Hubris

There was a buzz in the college about the upcoming marketing exam.

Makrand Ghatge, Atul's self-proclaimed close friend (one-sided) declared, "*Atlya*[5] is the marketing whiz in our class; he is going to crack the exam today."

"Wow Atul, you watched three movies back to back on the eve of the marketing exam?" Divyankar cried out with a hint of jealousy. Divyankar Dey, or DD channel, a term coined by Atul, was Atul's classmate and competitor; a presumptuous all-knowing *Bong*, who generally had an opinion on every god *damn* thing under the sun.

"*Atlya*, I am glad that I am sitting next to you in the exam. You will pass me your notes, *na*? After all, we are *chaddi buddies,* right?" implored Makrand. Few things irritated Atul more than being called *Atlya*, hence Makrand's plea was ignored.

---

[5] Nomenclature technique adopted by 'close' friends wherein the primary name is cut into half and 'ya' is added at the end. Commonly observed in Maharashtra.

"Hiiii Atul, can you guide me? I am *sooo* confused!" Shivani Laxmi cooed to Atul. Shivani was the class hottie, with a soft corner for guys with good grades. Atul and DD often competed for Shivani's charms, with DD frequently having the upper hand with his deceptive 'oh so intelligent and sensitive looks'. But this was Atul's moment and he was going to make the most of it.

"Of course, it will be my pleasure, Shivani. Err... how about we go for dinner after the exam?" asked Atul. While the question was posed at Shivani, the gaze centered on DD.

"Sure," said Shivani coyly. Atul had hit paydirt. If looks could kill, DD would have been booked under IPC 302.

Atul had built up quite a reputation in his college. College legend has it that Professor Joginder Bhat would get the shivers whenever Atul raised his hand in class to ask a question or to make a point. The presentation of the question itself (which was to the entire class, not just the professor), was a masterful demonstration on the usage of the English language, with most of the classmates scrambling to google the words on their smartphones. Atul would patiently wait for a few moments for his question to sink in and then turn his attention to the professor, who looked like he had been hit by a meteor. Just when the professor was about to open his mouth to reply, Atul would give a comprehensive reply to the question, in a brilliant fifteen-minute monologue, for the benefit of the professor and classmates. Atul knew the subject like the back of his hand. He believed that the entire marketing concept could be crystallized in terms of a technical formula $3Cs + 4Ps + STP$[6]. Towards the latter part of the marketing course, the professor would ignore Atul's raised hands. Angered by the consistent snubs, Atul bunked the

---

[6] Formula not approved by Kotler and hence not found in any of his books. You want to know what the formula means? Will let you know once I remember.

subsequent extra classes conducted by the professor to complete the course.

How did I know so much about Atul? That's because *I am Atul Malvankar,* heralded by many[7] as a likely worthy successor to Philip Kotler[8]. I never blow my own trumpet, but I can't gag others' mouths, can I?

Sitting in the examination hall, trying to focus on the upcoming marketing exam, I was finding it difficult to stifle my yawns. I had stayed up until early morning to watch five movies…a kind of a new dorm record. I felt lucky today, this was going to be too easy. It was going to be an open book exam, but referring books during an exam would be too time consuming, and was against my style. While the exam itself would be for two hours, I promised myself that I would be out of the examination hall in half the time. I glimpsed at DD, who had opened up five textbooks filled with multi-coloured separators, and one note book on his table. He was alternating between stealing glances at Shivani and checking up on me surreptitiously. What a loser!

Shivani, looking as hot as ever, seemed relatively relaxed; she was giving me the thumbs up sign. I reciprocated with a huge smile and two thumbs up signs, when I was sure DD was looking in my direction. I then looked at Makrand, who was offering fervent prayers to an idol of lord Ganesha kept on his table. As I surveyed the examination hall, I noticed rows of anxiety ridden faces chatting nervously with each other. I couldn't help a smug smile; *after all, marketing was an art, you either had it in you or you didn't.* I began to envision a red carpet welcome *(for me)* by Ramdev Baba at Patanjali, my dream company.

---

[7] At least two persons thought so; 1) My classmate Makrand Ghatge 2) My mother.

[8] Don't know Philip Kotler? Good for you. Kotler's books have been recommended by body building experts.

My dream was interrupted by the dowdy looking examination invigilator, who had walked into the room, clutching onto a bunch of huge packets. She had a forbidding demeanour; the class went into instant silence mode.

The invigilator wasted little time in issuing exam conduct rules to the students, opening the bulky packages, and extracting the contents. She studied the papers for a few moments and began to distribute them to the seated students. I thought I saw a fleeting smile across her face. My long distance vision could sense that something was not right! I got my copy from the invigilator a few moments later and my eyes almost popped out from their sockets!

The question paper was not a single sheet; it was a full-fledged book! I tried to count the pages 1-2-3-4, and then I simply flipped to the last page. The case study spanned 102 pages! There were ten separate annexures towards the end. My heart started palpitating exponentially; my hands and forehead had begun to perspire profusely. I could feel a pounding headache coming on. Hands trembling, I read the instructions enunciated by Prof Joginder Bhat on the top page.

Instructions

1. *Skim through the case study quickly (and we mean quickly).*
2. *Read the questions carefully (but quickly).*
3. *Read the case study in more depth now (but as quickly as possible).*
4. *Answer the questions (quickly, before time runs out).*
5. *Total time — 2 hours.*

You may use your textbook, notes, laptop during the exam. The only things not allowed are tips / guidance / notes from fellow classmates.

All the best for the exam.

I did some mental math. It would take me 5 minutes to read 1 page, 102 pages = 510 minutes or close to 9 hours! &%$#@**&%% ^%$#&%**!

I ignored the instructions and decided to read the questions first.

1. If you were the marketing manager of the company, how would you have arrived at the optimal marketing mix? What would be the ROI of this mix? Explain your calculations. (Tip: You can refer my notes given to you during my extra classes).
   *(ROI? Surely the prof doesn't mean return on investment? Is this a marketing or finance exam? Damn *&^%$#$ S&^%*)*

2. Determine customer lifetime value for each customer segment, including the ones not considered by the company management. Based on your calculations, which segment would you recommend? (Tip: You can refer my notes given to you during my extra classes).
   (Customer lifetime value? What on earth is that?)

3. Refer Annexures 3, 4, 6a and 7b. What should be the price and features offered to the targeted customer segment? Use conjoint analysis. (Tip: Use the CJA software that you would have downloaded during my extra classes).
   *(Hey, that's hitting below the belt! Conjoint Analysis was never part of the syllabus! *&^%$#$ S&^%**&%$)*

4. Would it be worthwhile to have a digital marketing plan complementing the traditional marketing plan? Can you formulate this digital marketing plan? (Tip: You can refer my notes given in my extra classes).
   *(Damn extra classes again? *&^%$#$ S&^%**&%$&^%)*

5. Hope you have read the book 'What the Customer Wants' by
    Anthony Ulwick (which I had strongly recommended during
    my extra classes). What would have been Ulwick's approach to
    the marketing problem in the case study?
    (Who is this Ulwick fellow now? Ullu da pattha. As if the books by
    Kotler were not enough, the prof wanted us to read one more by another
    author? *&^%$#$ S&^%**&%$&^%#@!*****beep beep beep
    beep).

I had to read and re-read the five questions multiple times, just to
allow them to sink in. At that moment, I did not hate anyone in the
world more than Prof Joginder Bhat.

I began the arduous task of reading the case study. The fellow
who had written the case study was perhaps aiming for the Nobel
prize in literature. I couldn't make out what the *numbskull* was trying
to say. Makrand kept distracting me, whispering incessantly, to pass
my answer sheet. I wanted to bonk him on the head, but ignored
him for now. I stuck to my task and plodded on, highlighting key
sentences in the case study with a yellow marker. I gave a sigh of
relief once I reached my first milestone – page no 25. However
relief was supplanted with horror when I saw my watch. One hour
gone, one hour remaining; 175 pages yet to be read. Unfortunately,
I couldn't remember any of the contents of the first 24 pages. Panic
began to set in.

I took a look around the hall to see how others were faring.
Makrand had the look of a drowning victim, desperately seeking
my rescue. Too bad, I had to think of how I could save myself first. I
looked at DD, who appeared to be writing some kind of a thesis. His
pen never left his paper, even as he kept asking for multiple answer
sheets from the invigilator. *The idiot! Did this fellow think he was going*
to get marks by the kilo? Here I was, sweating to fill a single A4 sheet!
I would have given a limb and an eye to know what that idiot was

scribbling on those sheets. I then looked in the direction of Shivani, who looked bewildered. She happened to look in my direction at the same time and signalled for help. She looked disappointed when I hung my head in shame. I wish the earth could have swallowed me at that very moment. Then Shivani looked at DD, who had raised his head for yet another answer sheet supplement. DD immediately seized the situation and gleefully handed one of his answer sheets to a grateful Shivani, behind the invigilator's back. *Bloody opportunist!*

Desperate times called for desperate measures. There was no point wasting time reading the remainder of the case study. I wrote my first line on the answer sheet:

'Marketing can be crystallized in terms of the following formula 3Cs+ 4Ps + STP'.

It was important to begin with a flourish and impress upon the professor the depth of my empirical knowledge, even though he had not asked for it. I then read each question again, closed my eyes, meditated for a couple of minutes before jotting down whatever came to my mind. These were inspired moments, as I began to define the key concepts stated in every question. My inspired answers were as follows:

1. ROI – An investment linked concept. The elusive idea that everyone talks about and wants but few have a clue.

2. Customer segment – You get a complete cake and cut into many different slices so that everyone can eat. Similarly, marketing guys slice and dice customer into various segments so that they can be eaten, I mean catered to by different companies. Like they say, 'no one size fits all'. Only the smart marketing guys are aware of such customer segments, never the not so smart customers themselves. Some might argue that each customer is different from the other, but they can keep arguing till the cows come home. There are some who argue that segmentation is not a good idea; the debate rages on.

3. Conjoint analysis. One makes two to three different types of analyses, joins them to make a conjoint analysis statement, and make it more comprehensive. A very useful analytics tool. (Note: would appreciate it if you could give me a couple of extra marks for using the word 'analytics').
4. Digital marketing plan – same thing as traditional, only in digital format and with generous doses of google.
5. Ulwick – The book 'What Customers Want' sounds similar to the movie 'What Women Want'. I haven't heard about Ulwick but I know about an Ulwe node in Navi Mumbai. Perhaps it is named after Ulwick? Nice place, incidentally.

Finally, I had some ink on my answer sheets! I had used my foresight to leave sufficient space between answers in order to fill matter later on.

'*Rrrrrrriiinnnnnnnnggggg*'

It was the alarm bell. "Last 10 minutes. Hurry up!" the invigilator yelled.

My heart threatened to jump out of my chest. Like a person possessed, I began to scrawl furiously in the open spaces between the answers, repeating the question below each answer. Using my presence of mind, I took due care in changing key words and phrases so that it would seem original and highlighting them using my yellow marker. I also quoted copiously from the highlighted texts in the case study (*in handwriting difficult to comprehend for most human beings, including myself*).

'*Rrrrrrrrrrrrriiiiiiiiiiiiiiinnnnnnnnnnnnnngggggggggggggggggggg*'

It was the final bell as the invigilator announced loudly, "Time's up. Stop writing and submit your papers."

"I said stop writing, Atul!" the invigilator barked, tapping her toes in irritation. I ignored her warning and continued to write even as all other students submitted their papers and streamed out of the exam hall. I was the sole student remaining.

"Two minutes more, ma'am. *Please,*" I pleaded with the invigilator, hoping to melt her heart with my funeral face.

The invigilator ignored me, packed the sheets and began to walk out. In desperation, I wrote in big bold letters at the beginning and end of my answer sheet 'MERCY'. I picked my incomplete work of art, ran behind the angry invigilator and begged her to accept my answer sheet. She gave me a frosty look and after some heart stopping moments, took the paper. My agony had finally come to an end.

As I exited the hall slowly and dejectedly, I noticed Charanjit (another classmate) and DD in animated conversation. Some students were celebrating for reasons best known to them. Morons! Makrand had slumped in a lone corner, apparently waiting for me. I tried to make a stealthy exit.

"Hey Atul! Man, you were writing way past the deadline…you must have cracked the paper today, right?" It was Charanjit who had spotted me.

Mind your own business, silly duffer!

I put an effort to smile, but didn't say anything.

I overheard DD jabbering away to a few classmates. "That was one hell of an easy paper. The case study had been discussed during the extra classes. Most of the answers were in the notes from the extra classes. Blah… blah…blah…blah…"

How about me putting some chili powder on your tongue right now? Bloody showoff!

I was getting a severe headache and tried to slink away. Makrand got up and followed me without invitation.

"Do they give any marks for cleanliness? I just submitted a totally blank answer sheet," sighed Makrand.

I almost fell sorry for Makrand. *Almost.*

I tried to locate Shivani; she would be a sight for sore eyes and a beaten ego. But she was nowhere to be seen. I dialled Shivani's number on my cellphone. One ring, two rings, three rings...a dozen rings. I tried over half a dozen times, but Shivani didn't pick up my call. Finally I got a beep on my cellphone. It was a message from Shivani.

Don't bug me. I am busy right now. And yes, forget about having dinner today or any other day. I have other commitments.

Et tu, Brutusini? Exit Atul, enter DD. Thank you very much Prof Joginder kamina Bhat.

I mentally toyed with the idea of filing a written complaint to higher authorities against *Prof Joginder bloody Bhat* for
- Mental torture *(anxiety, panic attacks)*.
- Physical torture *(eyes and brain were hurting)*.
- Discrimination and unfair practices by setting questions from extra classes only.
- Posing out of syllabus questions.

The turmoil was raging inside me; I had to find some way to flush the day's events from my system. Makrand seemed to read my thoughts when he proposed, "*Atlya*, let's grab some beers. We can then make a bonfire and burn the question paper. *Swaha!* What do you say?"

For once, I didn't mind being called *Atlya*. Come to think of it, there was a ring of caring and closeness in the name. The idea of burning the paper appealed to me; it would be *our* silent protest against the unjust system.

"Sure, *Makya*." I replied, adopting the 'ya' technique for the first time. Makrand was pleasantly surprised at the reciprocity.

We smuggled a few beers, went to the hostel terrace and lit a small fire using leaves and twigs. Makrand took a couple of beer bottles, opened the caps and offered one bottle to me. We clinked our bottles and exclaimed in unison, "*Cheers!*"before taking swigs of the chilled beer.

Makrand took out his question paper and put in the fire, simultaneously gulping down his beer.

"Down with Prof Bhat, down with Marketing, down with Kotler. Long live our friendship!" bellowed Makrand. We clinked our beer bottles again.

It was my turn. I took out the paper from my bag and was about to put it into the fire, when something caught my eye, freezing me to the core. My body trembled as my brain went numb.

It was my answer sheet!

Chance Encounter

*D*amn! *Damn! Damn!* Murphy's Law was in full effect. First of all, my moronic client had called an emergency meeting on a holiday. I tried to plead, cajole, persuade, coax, but it all came to naught when the irritating bugger threatened to cancel the contract. Second of all, my good for nothing travel agent could not get a flight ticket for me, on a sector with an average occupancy level of barely 25%! I had to settle for a bloody train ticket, that too second class A/C.

Me, Sushant Gade, the director of a Rs 10 crore company, travelling by train! I know the turnover might seem a little small, but air travel is my rightful entitlement. What the *&%$@! If the company CEO ever got to hear of this, *which I am sure that the ba*&^%$ would come to know*, he would expect me to travel by train in future also. Third of all, my heart almost leapt out from my chest having to navigate one of the worst traffic jams in life, sprint more than hundred metres in my new formal shoes, as I attempted to catch the train. It was a successful attempt in the end, as the train was late by a couple of hours. Thank god for the Indian Railways.

Was Mr Murphy done with me? No sir, he was just getting warmed up. Whilst trying to jump into my train compartment along with my luggage, a duffer crashed into me from nowhere. In an instant, I found myself writhing in pain on the platform, my luggage strewn all around me. I opened my mouth to hurl the choicest of abuses, when I noticed that the duffer was a 'she', not a 'he'. The lady was sporting a black sports cap and a rather largish pair of glares.

At night? How dumb could one get?

She had donned a pair of casual denim jeans with a bluish, floral crepe top and a stylish leather jacket. I would have continued to mutter curses under my breath, had the lady not apologized to me. The lady offered me a hand to help me on my feet, but I rebuffed her and focused on getting my dispersed luggage from the railway platform into the train compartment. Once I had got everything inside including myself, I calmed down a little.

"Thank ya," said a female voice in a heavy set American accent, from behind me. It was that lady again.

"*Hmmmph,*" I snorted, confused as to why she was thanking me. Then it dawned on me as I counted the number of luggage pieces; the number seemed to be unusually high. In my agitated state of mind, I had loaded the lady's luggage also into the compartment by mistake. I flirted momentarily with the thought of throwing her luggage out again. Instead, I ignored her and searched for my berth. I was happy to discover that I had a lower side berth, which meant an exclusive window seat. *The cloud did have a silver lining.* I dragged my luggage to my berth, and headed towards the washroom to freshen myself. The mental and physical stress of the day had taken a toll on me, I wanted to have a quick dinner and call it a night.

When I returned to my seat, lo and behold, it was no longer available. The lady in the black cap and dark curtains in front of her eyes had perched herself cozily on it as if she had been born on it.

I stood rooted to the spot, seething with rage. After some time, when the lady finally noticed me, she enquired in an infuriatingly cheerful tone, "Howdy dere again, ya needed somethin'?"

I couldn't decide which was more irritating, the fact that the lady had usurped my window seat or her fake American accent.

"Yes, my seat please, which you have encroached upon. This is my ticket, A-6 is clearly written on it, see? " I waved my ticket in front of her face indignantly and asked, "Can I see your ticket please?"

"Ooh, am so sorry. My bird number is A-5. I love a window seat, ya see. Do ya mind takin another seat? I would really appreciate it."

"No, I don't see. And yes, I do mind. First of all, it is berth number, not bird number. Moreover, this is my seat; your berth is the one above mine. If you want a window seat, why don't you occupy another seat over there? This train's almost empty." I pointed to another window side berth on the opposite side.

"Oh, no problem at all. Sorry for botherin ya." The lady moved immediately.

Good riddance! Finally some peace. The train was about to start.

"Ain't this exciting?" The lady cooed from the adjacent seat. I ignored her.

The lady persisted. "Do ya travel by train often or is this ya first time?"

What was with this lady, didn't she catch hints? Okay, she asked for it.

"Not really, I travel by train regularly and even have a monthly pass. As a matter of fact, Indian Railways has dedicated this seat for me. Why, is this your first time?" I asked sarcastically.

"Yes, this is muh first time in an Indian train," the lady replied coyly.

Sure, and I was born yesterday. You can stop with the lapetaoing[9], lady.

"And where are you from? America?" I asked mockingly.

"Oooh! Indians are so intelligent. How did ya guess?" the lady chirped. The lady then proceeded to take off her dark curtains and

---

9   Colloquial for faking

sports cap, revealing a young woman in her mid 20s with fair skin, steaming blue narrow eyes, plumpish cheeks, cropped wavy auburn hair.

Maybe that accent was real after all.

"I uhh... uhh..." I looked around me, trying to cook up something. "Your glares, they are made in USA, aren't they?"

"Oh these? I actually bought them in Mumbai. Hahaha."

"Yes, hahaha." I mirrored.

The lady then extended her hand towards me and said, "Jen."

I immediately folded my hands and said, "Namaste. But my name is not Jen. It is Sushant."

The lady did not take offence at her hand being rebuffed. She folded her hands likewise and giggled. "Jen is muh name actually. Namaste Sushante. Say, that's rhymes, don't it?"

"Yes, it does," I said wearily, not wanting to explain and encourage further conversation. To drive the point home, I extracted a Steig Larsson paperback from my suitcase titled, *The Girl with the Dragon Tattoo,* and switched on the reading lamp near the headrest. The train had started pulling away from the station.

Barely had the train left the station, when Jen said, "Ain't it a little hot in here?"

I looked up from the cover page of my novel and said with a straight face, "You can always open the windows, you know."

Jen looked at me, puzzled, before breaking out into a grin.

"Aah, joke, joke."

I rolled my eyes and turned to the first page in my novel, when Jen spoke up yet again. "Dat's a Steig Larsson novel, ain't it? The story is about—"

I cut her off immediately. "It's about some Chinese dragons who invade Dubai and South Africa, until they are finally tamed by a girl who makes tattoos on these dragons."

"Uh uh... sure, if ya say so. I was gonna say dat dey are makin a motion picture on the book and ..."

"Yes, yes, how exciting. Now, can I read the book please?"

Jen's face fell. She said apologetically. "Of course. Am I disturbin ya?"

I had barely turned to page one, when Jen spoke up again, "Ahem. Sorry for botherin you again. Can I axe you where the batroom is?"

I looked at Jen and said pointedly. "I don't know where the batroom is, but the washroom is ten steps away, near the compartment entrance."

"Thank ya so much," replied Jen and left.

I threw away my book; reading was next to impossible with such frequent interruptions. I decided that it was time to have my packed dinner and go off to sleep. Removing my stainless steel tiffin box from my suitcase, I began to open the plastic cover. The tiffin was still hot, great! There was steaming rice and dal. The yummy aroma wafted through the compartment, making me feel even hungrier. The highlight of the contents was a pair of huge, yummy, soft *gulab jamuns,* beckoning me to devour them. I had to act quickly before Jen returned to her seat. I started wolfing down the dal rice combo so that I could get to the gulab jamuns in a jiffy.

Alas, I was not quick enough. Food still stuffed in my mouth, Jen walked in from the washroom. She sniffed at the air and remarked. "Woww, dat's something. Ya know, I just *love* Indian food," said Jen, rolling her tongue and fixating her gaze on the two gulab jamuns.

I shifted my tiffin closer to me, smiled at Jen and continued eating. If Jen thought that I was going to share my tiffin, she was so sadly mistaken.

And then she made the dreaded request. "Do ya mind, if I try one of these? Dey look exotic."

Ha lady, no way. Go fly a kite. I quickly popped one of the gulab jamuns into my already stuffed mouth and shook my head violently to signal to Jen that I didn't want to share.

Jen looked at me, smiled and then did the unthinkable. She reached out to my tiffin, grabbed the gulab jamun and inserted it into her mouth.

"Mmmmmmmm, dis is one amazing thin'. It is a little too sweet, but it's fantastic. Thank ya so much. What are dey called?"

How dare she! I looked at Jen with daggers in my eyes but was unable to say anything with my mouth full. Then it struck me, Jen might have misread my head shaking signal for a 'yes'. *Stupid American.*

"They *were* called gulab jamuns. By the way, you know it's not healthy to share a stranger's food."

"Ya ain't a stranger, ya muh friend now, Sushante."

Just then, a couple of youths of unequal heights, in their early twenties, unshaven and wearing flimsy cooking aprons, walked into the compartment. The taller guy was sporting an earring in one ear and was carrying an assorted bundle of food trays, stacked one over the other. The shorter guy bore a prominent stubble and flaunted a pad and a pen. It was evident that he was the boss, as he was handling the money.

"*Khaana bolo khaana. Garma garam badiya non-veg khaana bolo khaana.*"

Why were these idiots shouting when the entire compartment was almost empty? I covered my ears promptly. Spotting Jen, the two men immediately ignored me and focused their energies on her.

"Food, madam? Very hot, very tasty, delicious Indian food."

Jen seemed to evince interest in the sales pitch. "How much?" she enquired.

"No problem madam. Food eat first, pay later." The leader didn't even wait for Jen's reply as he motioned his assistant to hand over one of the plates to Jen.

"Thanks man. Can I get ya one plate too, Sushante?" Jen looked at me and asked me. I remembered that the nodding of my head had taken on a different meaning earlier, so I simply replied, "No, thank you, Jen. But I must warn you. This food is spicy and unhygienic."

The leader of the two men became agitated on hearing this. He said angrily, *"Sir, aap thoda chup rahenge, kya? Madam khaana khane chahti hai, toh aapko kya problem hai?"*

"Hey Sushante, relax. I can handle Indian food, okay?"

The assistant handed over the plate to Jen promptly before I could open my mouth to protest. The two men disappeared almost immediately from the compartment after handing over the dinner plate. Jen took off the aluminum foil. La voilà, there were three desiccated *chappatis* in one corner. A second corner had a yellow fluid which looked like filtered dal (*without the dal*); there was rice hiding in the third corner garnished by one slice each of a dehydrated tomato and a starved onion ring. A muddy looking concoction was flowing in the remaining corner, which I guessed was the non-vegetarian fare.

Jen sniffed at her food and said to me, "Dis smells darned good. Ya sure, you don't wanna try some, Sushante?"

I shrugged my shoulders and said, "No, thank you. And good luck."

Jen dug into her food with a sorry pair of plastic spoon and fork, which had been packed separately. With every morsel of food she popped into her mouth, she licked her lips, made some silly '*mmmm*' sounds. Either Jen was an excellent actress or plain dumb. By the time she got to the non-veg fare, tears had begun to flow from her eyes. Frequency of licking had reduced considerably; the orgasmic sounds and rolling of the eyes had stopped completely.

"Are you all right?" I asked Jen out of concern.

Jen wiped her tears with her left hand and gave me a thumbs up, "Yeah, yeah, food's a little spicy, but duhlicious. I can handle it. But muh belly is full, am gonna stop now. Excuse me; I gotta rush to the batroom." Jen then placed the half eaten plate below her seat and rushed to the washroom. I continued reading.

Jen had not returned, and it had been a while. Anxious, I decided to go to the washroom and check. I couldn't spot her outside the washroom, which meant Jen had either fallen off the train or she was still closeted inside the washroom; the latter scenario being more likely. There were violent sounds emanating from the washroom; it was Jen alright. I knocked. Jen opened the door in a while. She looked spent and exhausted.

"What happened? Are you okay?" I asked. It was a stupid question, I realized belatedly.

Jen smiled weakly and replied, "I guess the stuff I ate had something real strong and I ain't ready yet to handle train food. I am gonna be okay, don't worry...awwwwkkkkk."

Jen turned towards the basin again to puke.

"Awwwwk...aawwwwkkkkk...awwwwwwwwwwwwwwk."

That did it, a surge of undigested food remnants came gushing forth from Jen's mouth right into the basin. I felt like throwing up myself.

Jen began to recover once the villainous contents had been ejected from her system. We had barely gone back to our seats when the train food couple reappeared. The shorter guy looked at Jen and flashed a fake smile at her, exposing his betel-stained teeth.

"Hello madam. You liked dinner?" Before Jen could reply, the fellow said, "One thousand rupees, madam. Special price, only for you."

I was about to explode, but I controlled myself. "*Ek toh ladki marte marte bachi hai tumhara ghatiya khana kha kar, upar so tum dono ne achhi khasi loot macha rakhi hai?*" I was trembling in fury.

The two guys ignored me, which infuriated me even more.

I tapped the shorter one on his shoulder and said, "*Main tum dono se baat kar raha hoon.*" I still did not elicit any reaction from the duo. Jen had already extracted the money from her purse and was about to hand it over, when I stopped her. "No Jen, do not give these thugs any money."

This time, there was a reaction. *"Saab, kyon dhanda khoti kar rahe ho? Madam jab khushi khushi paise de rahi hai, toh aapke baap ka kya ja raha hai?"* the shorter guy said angrily.

I took a deep breath, clicked a picture of the duo on my cell phone and said calmly, *"Baharwalon ko ch****** banana band kar. Ek minute aur khada raha yahan par, toh Facebook or Twitter par tum dono ki band bajwaoonga. Bhaag le yahan se."*

The duo moved away hastily, but not before issuing a warning of their own, that they would see me outside, etc., etc.

A perplexed Jen asked, "Wat was all dat about?"

"Nothing, I told the guys that they were like my younger brothers and that they should give you a 100% discount. They agreed."

"Really? Dat's incredible. By the way, wat is the meaning of ch******? Hear dat word a lot in India."

It was my turn to be perplexed. *"Uhh... errr...* it is a term that one uses to endearingly address others, very commonly used among friends."

Jen smiled warmly, "Okay, let me see if I get this right. Ch******, ch******, ch*******...you are a great ch******, you know."

I was stumped. "Good Jen, very good. So what brings you to India?" I asked, hastily changing topics. "Let me guess, a slum tour, Goa, ISKCON or reverse outsourcing?"

"Wat's reverse outsourcing?"

"Oh, that's simple. It's the opposite of outsourcing," I said eruditely.

"Oh no, no no. Am here only to see India. I hear that it is one hell of a beautiful country. Just last week, I saw the Taj Mahal. Wow, what a beautiful structure! The whiteness, the symmetry and all. But ya already know that, don't ya?"

"Yes, I have seen the pictures on the net."

"Ya haven't actually seen the Taj Mahal? Ya pullin a gag on me?"

"Not yet, but I have seen the Grand Canyon in USA. That's quite amazing too. Have you seen it?"

"Nah, ain't got the time to see it yet. But surely ya can't compare the Taj Mahal to the Grand Canyon. Taj Mahal is way up the list. Can ya imagine the king's love for his queen? How romantic!"

"Huh, I don't see what the big deal is about an emperor who built one mega monument for one wife and none for his other wives. How unfair is that? And did you know that this bozo had the architects' hands cut off so they could never build another one like it? On the other hand, the Grand Canyon is god's own creation. No politics, no discrimination, no slave labour. Pure natural beauty."

"Ya are speakin too fast and too much. Gotta slow down, can't understand ya."

I calmed myself down, thought for a few seconds and said slowly, "That was too long for me to remember and repeat."

Jen banged her fist on her seat and declared, "I am tellin ya, the Taj Mahal is the number one wonder of the world. Check Google."

I was not to be left behind. I too banged my fist on the window and declared, "I don't care what Google says. For me, Grand Canyon is number one."

"Ticket please." It was the train ticket collector (TC), who had interrupted our debate. He was dressed in a black jacket, a wrinkled black tie, black trouser and black shoes. To balance all the blackness, he had worn a white shirt.

I promptly showed the printout of my ticket to the TC, which he scrutinized very carefully. Trifle disappointed that everything was in order, he then asked Jen for her ticket. Jen rummaged her purse and trouser pockets but was unable to locate her ticket. She apologized profusely to the TC. The TC loosened his tie, narrowed his eyes and studied Jen.

"Where are you from?" asked the TC.

"USA," replied Jen.

"Oh, I thought you were from America. Anyway, you are a guest in our country and I will let you go. But you must be more careful the next time."

"Thank ya so much sir, you are a ch******."

The TC stood frozen in his tracks, not believing what he had just heard. Neither did I.

"What was that again, eh?" asked the agitated TC.

Before Jen could repeat, I spoke up. "*Sir, uski bhaasha thodi kamzor hai, isiliye kuch bolti hai, kuch aur sunai deti hai.Woh keh rahi hai ki aap bahut acche hain.*"

The suspicious TC did not seem to buy my explanation entirely, but he did not pursue the matter and left.

"Great guy. But why was he so unhappy?" Jen observed.

I turned to Jen and said, "His life is all black and white, he could do with more colour. But you should use that 'C' word very sparingly, only when you are close friends with someone. On second thoughts, better not to use it at all."

"Hmmm, okay. Can I axe ya wat do ya do for a livin, Sushante?"

"I am the director of an elastic manufacturing company supplying elastic threads to undergarment companies. We also export to over forty-six countries, including USA," I said proudly.

"Hmmmm. So, if my bra falls off for some reason, I know whom to call?" Jen asked with a mischievous twinkle in her eye.

I was taken unawares. "I, err… uhhhh…."

Jen laughed and said, "Relax, just pullin your leg. I don't wear bras."

Looking at my shocked expression, Jen laughed harder and said, "Ya fell for dat one too, eh? Ya not gonna axe me wat I do?"

"What do you do, Jen?"

"Aah, I do plenty stuff. I am the lead singer in a band, do sum paintin here and there and a little bit of actin when I get the time. Ya like movies, Sushante?"

"I hate films in general, but I do watch the odd Hollywood one."

Jen straightened up and asked, "Oh yeah? Which one?"

I scratched my head, "Uhhh, let me remember something that had to do with Newton's laws and an apple…what was the damn name?"

"*Gravity?*" Jen suggested.

"Yes, that's it. Liked the movie, great special effects, good acting by the heroine. Movie got many Oscars, but the heroine missed out. Felt sad for her."

"Yeah. Sandra is a fine actress, but sometimes she can be such a b****!"

"Sandra who?"

"Sandra Bullock, the lead actor of *Gravity.*"

"You know Sandra Bullock?" I queried incredulously.

"I wish, darlin! Get all my info from the tabloids back home."

"Then there was another movie I liked, where this fellow is stranded in Mars…let me try to remember the name of the movie…"

Jen tapped her fingers on the seat patiently and suggested helpfully, "*Martian?*"

"Yes, you are fantastic with names, Jen. That hero, Demon something, was fabulous. That movie also won a few Oscars."

Jen seemed to disagree. "Dunno. Nowdays, Oscars got no value. I mean, if a movie gets an Oscar, just sum stones flyin here and dere in space or bcos someone grows potatoes out of human crap den sumthin is very wrong. Where's the actin? It's all technology."

"Well, I liked *Martian*. But I agree with you, there are a few overrated movies and actors. I saw this movie *American Wrestle*,

couldn't figure out what was going on. Then there was *Oscar Games*.
I had to switch off the tv after watching it for thirty minutes. I got
a headache."

Jen sighed and said, "Ya mean *American Hustle* and *Hunger Games*."

"Yes, yes. Bad story, bad acting, a total waste of time. There was
one actor in both movies – she was particularly terrible."

"Ya talkin about Jennifer Lawrence? Surely, she can't be dat bad;
she won an Oscar and all."

"I thought you said that you didn't believe in the Oscars?"

"Yeah, well…"

"Anyway, who cares? Say, what time is it now? Shouldn't we be
hitting the bed?"

"Awww… so early ? It's only midnight. I wanna talk more."

"We could have, but I need to get up early. You also try to get
some sleep."

Jen sighed and said, "Okai. Can ya wake me up in the mornin?
I am a late riser."

The train was now roaring ahead with gusto. We both took to
preparing our beds and lay down. Barely ten minutes later, I could
hear soft snoring sounds from the other bed. Lucky Jen! I twisted
and turned in my bed, but could not sleep. My mind kept shifting
back to my conversation with the American, her quest for adventure
and her infectious enthusiasm. I got up to go to the washroom. As
I arose from my seat, I noticed that Jen was curled up like a baby.
She was fast asleep, but seemed to be shivering. Her blanket was
missing. I went back to my berth, took my blanket, tiptoed back to
Jen's berth and covered her ever so gently with it. Thereafter I went
to the washroom, returned to my berth, took out my novel and
switched on the reading light. I was now on page fifty one.

"*Sir, sir, wake up!*" I could feel someone shaking me, as I rubbed
my eyes. It was a newspaper boy.

"Sir, the train is going to reach the final station. Please get up.
Would you like to buy a newspaper?"

My head was still groggy, as my hands fumbled around clumsily. I discovered my novel lying next to me. It was half open, with page number fifty-one badly crumpled.

"Sir, newspaper?" The boy reminded. I nodded and exchanged a five-rupee note for the morning newspaper. Getting up from my berth, I stretched myself lazily. Then it struck me. *Jen!* I looked at the berth opposite mine; the blanket and the bedsheets were neatly folded and kept in a corner. There was no sign of Jen, she was gone. No greeting, no goodbye. Vamoose just like that!

I unfolded the newspaper. The front page headline was captioned, 'Leading Hollywood actress Jennifer Lawrence rumoured to be on a secret trip to India.'

I folded the newspaper again. The major newspapers were turning into tabloids these days, worth less than toilet paper. I decided to throw the newspaper in the trash bin and utilize the time in packing my bags and getting ready. I would have little time to waste, once my train reached its destination.

As I began to put on my shoes, a small yellow note fluttering out of my novel caught my eye. *What's that?* I picked it up. There was something scribbled on it in a feminine scrawl. Intrigued, I started reading.

It was a lovely experience getting to know you, Sushante. I am sorry that I couldn't say goodbye to you, didn't have the heart to wake you up. Hope we can meet again someday? By the way, I will be starring in the Hollywood movie — The Girl with Dragon Tatoo. Yes, the very book that you were reading. Please do watch it when it releases. Maybe you will change your mind about my acting skills. Love, Jennifer Lawrence.

PS: I agree with you, you can't beat the Grand Canyon. Either way, I win☺.

Avatar

My eyes were closed, but I could feel the sensuous soft touch of a woman's lips, pressing against mine. A mellifluous voice greeted me.

"Good morning, darling."

My eyes opened slowly; the woman of my dreams was sitting beside me. Eyes shaped like almonds, lush black hair like strands of silk flowing down the scalp of her head, neatly shaped eyebrows resembling the spread out wings of an eagle, sharp symmetrical nose, dimpled cheeks, slender neck, near perfect body curves, dimensions, etc., etc.

"Wakie wakie, Sid." More sensuous kisses followed on my nose, cheeks, ears, forehead and neck.

"Hey, hey! I am all awoken already."

Pulling her close to me, I closed my eyes, opened my mouth wide and waggled my tongue in sweet anticipation. However, she put her hand in front of my mouth and pushed it back.

"Don't be greedy. I have made some breakfast for you. Please have it *na*."

"But I am already having my breakfast—" I tried to pull her towards me again, in vain.

"Behave yourself, dear. You don't want to get late for office."

She placed a tray in front of me, containing a dish with four slices of bread with 90% burns, a multi-coloured omlette which had been torn brutally, accompanied by a bucket of black coffee which smelt and looked like varnish.

I looked at the spread and swallowed hard. "Looks delicious! You are a natural. I can barely wait to eat. Err, could you pack it in my tiffin? I will have it on the way."

"Nonsense dear, I want to feed you myself."

I do not know the idiot's name, who said that there is always a choice. By the time the torture had ended, I did not want to have breakfast in my life, ever again.

"What do you think of my plan, Siddharth? Can you make an estimate of the cashflow & IRR in the next couple of days? Siddharth? Hey, why are you making those funny faces?"

I was jolted out of my day dream by my boss's gruff voice. "*Uh, huh.*"

"What do you think of my plan, Siddharth?" asked my boss again.

I had absolutely no clue.

"Fantastic plan, sir! It will be a superhit. I will prepare the feasibility report in two days."

"Excellent."

I promptly typed out a message to my colleague, Amit Trivedi, who was sitting next to boss.

Hope you took notes, buddy. Will want to discuss the plan with you in depth after this meeting and get more details.

I received a message from Amit immediately.

Day dreaming again, eh? You owe me one more, man ☺. He was grinning.

Shut up! I texted back.

"What is the next item on today's agenda?" asked our boss.

"Tea break, everyone," interrupted a familiar, cheerful voice. And then she appeared in the meeting room, resplendent in her dark blue denims and an orange kurta. So simple, yet so elegant, as she brought in a tray of freshly brewed tea and snacks.

It was Devyani. The girl of my dreams!

The serious look on my boss's face metamorphosed into a smile. "*Arrey beta,* you could have asked Arun to get the tea."

I nodded my head in agreement, scrambled to get up from my seat, and take the tray from her delicate hands. Devyani smiled at me and motioned me to remain seated, before turning to her father.

"Papa, you forgot that you had sent Arun out to get the car repaired. Besides, serving tea is no trouble at all."

Amit looked at me amusedly and winked. I tried to kick him hard on his shin, below the table, but missed him, hitting my leg against the fat table leg instead.

"Owww."

Devyani placed the tea cups next to each one of us, and I noticed happily that she had given me the cup with tea filled to the brim. I was over the moon when she pulled up a chair next to me.

A couple of moments later, Devyani's brother Navin, a boy no older than fourteen years old, walked into the room accompanied by their mother. Navin pulled up a chair and sat close to me, whereas his mother sat down next to Amit. Navin raised his palm, to give me a high five. I looked at my boss; it was a delicate and awkward moment. My boss looked at me for a couple of seconds and then approved.

"It's okay. Go ahead!" I returned Navin's high five.

"We are trying to have an office meeting here, ma'am," said our boss in an exasperated tone.

"Sir, your business meetings will never end." Our boss and his wife addressed each other as ma'am and sir, for reasons best known to them.

"Have you informed the boys about the dinner tonight? Or have you forgotten as usual?"

Our boss, who was usually a stern, demanding professional, turned to jelly in front of his wife.

"How could I have forgotten, m'am? I told them today morning itself, isn't that so boys?"

Amit and I exchanged confused looks; no one had told us anything about a dinner invite. As bachelors, we were always amenable to food invitations – anything, anytime, anyplace, anybody.

"Yes ma'am. Sir told us about it in the morning," Amit replied, recovering.

"See, I told you."

"I will be making a special dish tonight," Devyani announced.

Amit and I exchanged glances again, alarmed. This exchange did not go unnoticed.

"No need to look so worried. My cooking skills are improving with each passing day, you know," said Devyani.

"I will be doing the bulk of the cooking. Is 8 p.m. okay with both of you?" Ma'am said.

"Yes, ma'am," replied our boss on our behalf.

"Not asking you, sir."

"Yes ma'am, it's fine."

"Good," said ma'am turning toward our boss before continuing, "Can you let the boys leave a little early today, please?"

"I'll try."

"No trying please. The boys should go early today, else dinner will get late."

"Yes ma'am," sighed our boss before muttering to himself. "Told corporate so many times that we should take a separate office, but no."

"Were you saying something, sir?" Ma'am asked.

"No, no, nothing at all. By the way boys, there will be drinks too," announced our boss with a twinkle in his eye. Ma'am seemed to be slightly annoyed, but she let it slide.

Two years had flown since my first day at the Technostat Indore branch, as a management trainee. This was my first job, right out of college. Technostat manufactured and marketed industrial machine tools. I had been deputed to Indore and assigned to my boss, Mr Balraj Soni, by the corporate office. My brief was simple: help my boss establish the branch office and grow operations. As revenues were low, my boss had been operating from a bungalow, which functioned as both residence and office. Built over twenty years ago, the expansive structure with six rooms, a kitchen, three washrooms and a compact well maintained lawn, had never been occupied by its owners, who were NRIs. Three rooms were allocated for office activities; my boss and his family stayed in the remaining three rooms. The total staff strength in the branch office was four, including Arun, the office boy. Amit Trivedi, originally from Gujarat[10] joined six months after me, making me the default senior management trainee. Our relationship gradually blossomed from colleagues to room partners, to save on rent.

Family interactions became inevitable at the residence cum office. My boss, Mr Balraj Soni, was a tough, respected but demanding professional, often driving me crazy. However, on the inside, he was a large-hearted man of simple tastes and an obliging mentor. His wife, Madhumita Soni, a chartered accountant by profession, had left her job years ago, to tend to the family. She was a no nonsense lady with an occasional acerbic tongue. But she pampered me and Amit, by chiding our boss when he worked us too hard or by cooking up delicious meals when we had to stay back late

---

[10] For academic purposes only, keeping in mind geographic interests of a few readers. I was from Jabalpur.

in office. Mr and Mrs Soni became our de-facto father and mother away from home.

Devyani, the elder of their two children, had just finished her graduation in Arts. Courteous, polite, elegant, charming, Devyani was also a brilliant student, having secured the top rank in the university. But she had weird goals in life, like writing a thesis on spirituality and the relevance of godmen, offering counselling for those with suicidal tendencies, volunteering for social service in Bangladesh and becoming a great chef. Notwithstanding her many talents, Devyani was a miserable cook, putting it mildly. I and Amit were the unfortunate guinea pigs for many of Devyani's culinary experiments. Despite all her faults, Devyani was drop dead gorgeous; my heart always skipped a beat when I saw her.

Devyani's brother Navin was a typical teenager – moody, inquisitive, impatient, and perennially fighting with his sister. I was his role model. *Surprise, surprise.* However, I almost came close to losing the title of role model, when I tried to help out Navin at the behest of Devyani in a science project competition at school. We attempted to build up a low cost ATM machine, but the damn thing malfunctioned from day one, refusing to spit out the notes. When I tried to use force, it tore up the notes. Navin had to withdraw his name from the competition. It was humiliating.

Amit and I were back at our shared dwelling in the evening. We were freshening up and getting ready for the dinner party, when Amit accosted me.

"Dude, what's your problem?"

"*Huhh?*"

"Why are you acting so loony and zonked out these days?"

Amit had taken me by surprise. I looked at him for a few moments before the words spilt out of my mouth automatically, "I love Devyani."

I put my hand to my mouth; it was too late as Amit looked at me in horror.

"Surely you are joking, right?"

"I, I, err…"

"Oh my god! Hooohoooo."

"Look Amit, you can't tell this to anybody. Please. I will be screwed!"

"Damn right, you are! You know that sir and ma'am treat us almost like their own children. At the very least, you could lose your job, perhaps with some thrashing thrown in. They might even call the cops!"

"Stop it, Amit. You are scaring me."

"Arrey, it's good to visualize all possibilities. Helps in planning counter measures, you know – like running away, finding another job, etc. But Sid, how can you even cultivate such thoughts? Devyani treats both of us like her brothers."

"But she already has a brother. Why does she need one more? No, no, I think that she also feels about me the same way that I feel for her."

"How can you be so sure?"

"All the little things that she does for me. Did you not see how she gave me the cup full of tea and how she sat beside me today?"

"Oh, c'mon Sid!"

"Then, there was the time she greeted me on my birthday and gave me a birthday gift as well?"

"Yeah, how can I forget? Your birthday was over more than a month ago, she got the date completely wrong. Besides, she couldn't return the gift also, it had been gifted to her from someone else. Don't look at me like that! I know because Navin told me."

"It's the thought that counts. Okay, how about this? She always greets me with a huge smile and laughs at all my jokes."

"Yeah, that bit *is* puzzling. Either she has a poor sense of humour, or perhaps she is just laughing at you."

"Haha, aren't you the funny one, Mr Amit Trivedi?"

"Look Sid, if you want to commit *hara-kiri*, go right ahead. But don't expect me to play any part in your one-sided love story, stranger."

"Amit, I need your help. Please. What should I do now?"

"Hmmm...why don't you share your feelings with her directly? If nothing else, you will save a lot of time."

"What if she rejects me?"

"I don't understand you. On the one hand, you say that she has feelings for you, and in the same breath, you say that she can reject you?"

"How do I share my feelings unless she is alone? She is always with her mother, brother or father at any point of time."

"Hmmm... a classic 'lack of guts' syndrome. Well, don't expect *me* to present your case to her."

"Do you think that I should write her a note?"

"Instead of a note, why don't you send her a text message instead? Much more efficient."

"Arrey, I don't have her mobile number. Even if I did, Navin is always fiddling with her phone. There is a real danger that he could see the message and announce it to the world. Besides, a note is more romantic. But what should I write?"

"I suggest you start off with 'Dear' and end with 'Love'. I am sure you will think of something to fill the easy middle part. Err, can we leave now? We might get late."

"Give me five minutes."

I tore off a sheet of paper from an unused notebook and began to think. Just when I needed my cognitive faculties the most, my mind went blank. I tried short breathing exercises, standing up, pacing up and down my room, jogging, but nothing worked. Not even a single word! After struggling for fifteen minutes, I had a flash of inspiration. Digging out a secret photograph of Devyani from my cellphone which I had taken from one of the family pics in the boss's residence, I looked at it and meditated. The thought tap finally uncorked, as I began to jot down the words.

Dear Devyani,

I hope you will not get cross with me when you read this note. It is not my intention to make you angry, so if you do get bugged, please forgive me. I have wanted to say something to you for a long time. I had to get it off my chest, otherwise I would have had a heart attack. Not literally, but figuratively speaking, that is.

"Hey Sid, hurry up, we are getting late. Your five minutes ended an hour ago!" Amit screamed.
"Five minutes more, please."

I consider myself lucky to have met such a Beautiful and Wonderful person as yourself (the capital B &W are deliberate). You are kind, generous, charming, etc., etc.(I am running out of adjectives here). I was attracted to you ~~like a moth to a flame and did not realize when I fell in love with you.~~
You might have some second thoughts / concerns over the following issues, so I thought I will address them here itself.

~~Some say that I am fat.~~ My fat to body mass ratio may be a little higher than average — I will buy a Madhavi Nadkarni diet and exercise CD and pledge to lose ~~10 kgs~~ ~~5 kgs~~ 3 kgs, ~~within 2 months,~~ after 2 months.

~~0   You might be worried that I have another girlfriend — I wish to assure you that I am a virgin and~~ I have been waiting for someone like you all my life.
~~0   You are more qualified than me.~~ I am planning to do higher studies.

"*&^%$#&^%$! Are you writing a book for her or what? If you aren't ready in the next five minutes as per Indian Standard Time, I am leaving!" It was Amit again, sounding pissed.

"Arrey, two minutes more only. Please wait na, Amit." I got back to writing the note once again.

Re-iterating my strong points, to help make up your mind;

1. *I have a good sense of humour and can make you laugh.*
2. ~~*I bathe twice a day*~~ *I give high priority to personal hygiene.*
3. *I wash my own clothes and keep the dishes in the sink after having my meal.*
4. *I am planning to buy a car* ~~*as soon as my loan gets approved*~~. *shortly.*
5. *I love candle light dinners. Everytime the light goes out in my house when having dinner, I use candles.*
6. *Etc., Etc. (I can add more points but then this list will become too long.)*

Sorry, but I have to rush now, there is an idiot who is sitting on my head. Want to end saying that I know that I love you. Once again, please don't get angry. I will wait for a favourable response.

In case you are having any negative thoughts or if there is any confusion, we can discuss it. Everything is possible through conversation and dialogue.

Siddharth

PS: It is my humble request that you do not share this note with your father or mother, and especially Navin.'

●

We were *only* an hour and half late, when we reached our boss's residence. Ma'am and Devyani had already started placing the dinner on the dining table. Not to be left out, boss had proactively opened the whisky bottle and kept it atop the small coffee table alongside three empty glasses. He did not look too happy with the waiting.

"Where did you boys get stuck?" Boss asked with a hint of irritation.

Before we could reply, ma'am announced, "Dinner's about to be served, everyone."

"But ma'am, we have not even had a sip yet. It will be an insult to the bottle if we sit down for dinner without ingesting a drop of alcohol."

"Okay, okay. But no more than two pegs, the doctor has told you strictly."

Boss muttered something in a low pitch. He poured a large peg of whisky into his glass, when ma'am wasn't looking. I followed suit. Amit simply poured some water into his glass on the pretext that he would be driving. *God bless him.*

I began to have a sip from my glass, when boss and Amit clinked their glasses and said, "Cheers." I withdrew my glass from my mouth hastily.

Devyani, dressed in an eye-catching yellow georgette lehenga choli, made an entry with a tray full of snacks in her dainty hands. As if looks were not enough to kill, Devyani had sprayed some kind of fragrance, which made me want to get really close to her. She was accompanied by Navin. I stood up immediately to offer Devyani a chair.

"Why are you getting up? Didi can sit on this extra chair," Navin remarked, pointing to an extra chair next to us. He promptly plonked himself on the extra chair.

Devyani smiled and informed me that she would have to help her mother with the dinner. The moment her back was turned, Amit looked at me and grinned. I swore at him under my breath.

"What's that, eh?" asked boss.

"Nothing sir, just telling Amit that sales have been good this year."

"Yes, yes. And you two boys have done well. But there is still a long way to go in terms of channel expansion."

I felt a poke in my ribs; it was Navin. "Do you have Pokemon Go on your mobile?" he whispered.

"I, uhh...what is Pokemon Go?"

"It's a game, where you see some Pokemon creatures in reality and capture them. Never mind. Do you have Temple Run 2? No? Candy Crush?No?"

"Er I, uh, may have Solitaire," I offered apologetically.

"Navin, why are you harassing Siddharth?" Boss reprimanded Navin.

"No sweat, I will take Didi's phone."

Devyani had already started placing dinner on the table. Noticing that she was alone, I mustered all my courage to walk up to her. My feet were trembling, but it was now or never.

"Are you feeling all right? You look positively ill," asked Devyani with genuine concern, as I stood next to her.

My heart was about to explode."I, uhh am okay," I croaked and gave a silly grin.

This is your chance.Why are you standing and grinning like an idiot? DO IT. Hand over the note right now.

"Here, try to a sample of this *moong dal halva*." Devyani offered me a bowl of the sweet. I took a huge spoonful of the contents into my mouth and almost spat it out immediately.

No, don't do it. It will be a mistake that you will regret for life.What if she reacts badly?What will happen to my career?

I chewed the food slowly but the taste didn't register in my brain. "It's very good," I lied.

Devyani was pleased. "Thank you. I made it."

Don't think so much. If you don't act now, you will regret all your life. Give her the note, DAMMIT.

My tongue was getting twisty, as I was gasping for words. My eyes fell upon a plate of vegetable salad kept on the table.

"That salad looks tempting. Nicely cut and arranged."

Moron. Ass. Duffer. Coward.

"Why don't you try some?" Devyani held out the plate.

"Maybe later, thanks. I, uh, wanted to—" My tongue froze again.

"Yes, Siddharth?"

Don't be a wimp. Tell her.

"What are your career plans?"

Pathetic man! Go drown yourself in chullubhar paani.

"Oh, I haven't thought about it as yet. Right now, I am just living life in the present."

I was struggling and tried to find an escape route.

"Uh… I will have to get back to Boss and Amit. Thank you once again for the delicious halva. I look forward to take multiple helpings during dinner."

With the conclusion of the scintillating conversation, I walked back to my seat, sad but relieved that my ordeal had ended.

I had barely placed my butt on my seat, when Amit whispered in my ears. "Back so quickly? You gave the note, kya?"

My downcast face said it all.

"Accha, why don't you try and slip the note into one of her books?"

"Which book? She reads tons of books. Perhaps I can plant it in her shoe?"

"Not bad. But be careful not to put it into her mom's shoe by mistake."

As if on cue, Deyvani's mom appeared at that moment and pulled up a chair next to us. I stared at her feet intently; she was not wearing shoes. Ma'am looked at our boss sternly. He became conscious of her gaze on him.

"This is my first glass only, I promise."

"I didn't say anything. But the colour of the drink in your glass is the same as the colour of the alcohol in the bottle."

"That's just the lighting effect, ma'am. Is dinner ready?" Boss asked, trying to change the topic abruptly.

Ma'am sighed. "I came to tell you all that dinner's ready. Hope you boys like it, it is simple and spartan fare."

All of us took seats next to the dinner table, with the glasses in our hands. There was *palak paneer, basmati rice, kabuli chole subzi, raita*, assorted Indian bread, Italian pasta, salad, and of course, *moong dal halva*.

"Man, we should have skipped both breakfast and lunch today," remarked Amit wryly to me.

Ma'am and Devyani began to serve the food onto our plates, ignoring our protestations of self help. They kept serving, ensuring that there was not a spot of visible empty space on our plates, and stopped only when we moved our plates away. Devyani gave me more than generous helpings of *moong dal halva,* much to my horror.

"Ma'am, the food is delicious. Is there any special occasion today?" Amit asked ma'am, as he helped himself to some basmati rice and chhole subzi.

"So you mean the food is not good on other occasions, *eh?*" Navin observed with a twinkle in his eye.

Amit ducked for cover. "No, no, I didn't mean that. I meant..." Devyani scowled at Navin.

"Can you pass me the *raita* please?" Boss asked absent-mindedly.

I took a huge helping of palak paneer into my mouth, as I passed the *raita* to my boss.

"Thank you, Amit. Sir has a surprise for one of you boys today. Sir?"

Boss withdrew the spoon filled with raita from his mouth and said blandly, "Ah yes. Siddharth, you are being promoted to assistant manager and transferred to corporate office. Congratulations, my boy." Having made the announcement, boss inserted the spoonful of raita back into his mouth.

I was speechless. Amit and Navin immediately rushed towards me to congratulate me. Devyani too walked up to me, smiled warmly, shook my hand, and said, "Many congratulations, Siddharth. You will now be the big man in corporate."

I finally found my voice. "But sir, I love it here. I mean, I thought I was doing quite well here. I appreciate the promotion and all, but what will I do in corporate office?"

Boss shrugged his shoulders and took another spoonful of raita into his mouth. "Well, you know how it is with those guys at the head office. It is almost impossible to debate logic with them when they have taken a decision. They insisted on bundling the transfer with your promotion. I didn't want to impede your career in any way."

"But sir, business is growing now. Don't you need me here?" I persisted.

"Nah, it's okay really. Amit has shaped up quite well, plus we are getting a couple of replacements."

Amit saw an opening and jumped in. "Sir, ahem, is there any possibility of me getting a promotion also?"

"Amit, in your case, there is both good news and bad news. The bad news is that we could give only one promotion this year at this branch, as per the quota system. The good news is that your promotion is assured next year, subject to your not leaving the company, of course."

Amit appeared to be placated by the reply.

I would have given my left arm to exchange places with Amit. Crestfallen, I shoved another big morsel of palak paneer into my mouth.

"Actually, there is one more occasion for celebration today," Ma'am spoke up again. "You see, our little daughter, who is not so little now, is about to get married."

I almost choked on my morsel of palak paneer.

"Excuse me?" I looked at Amit in horror.

"We fixed Devyani's marriage yesterday. The boy is Devyani's childhood friend and his parents are like family to us."

"But, but…have you asked Devyani about this? What about her future plans?" I began to protest. My dismay increased multifold when I noticed Devyani blushing. Tears had started flooding my eyes.

"Of course, Siddharth. We couldn't have done anything without Devyani's explicit consent. Panditji has given a *mahurat* six months from now. Both you and Amit must come for the wedding."

I had lost my appetite. This was all a bad dream which would end in the morning and then everything would be fine.

"That's great news. Congratulations, Devyani," Amit chirped.

I would have surely punched Amit, had he not been seated far away from me.

My nightmare was getting worse. It was as if the entire world was plotting to take me away from my Devyani.

"You will come to my wedding na, Siddharth?" Devyani asked me pointedly, flashing a sweet smile.

Oh, please cut the crap. Do you also want me to do the kanyadaan, while you are at it?

"I… I… will see." Keeping my emotions in check was becoming doubly hard with the alcohol inside me.

"Nothing doing, you will have to come to my wedding. No excuses," Devyani declared.

And then the dam burst. I broke down and began to sob loudly to everyone's bewilderment. Even Amit was taken aback by my extreme reaction. Ma'am shot an accusing look at sir.

"It's all your fault!"

"Hey, it was the corporate office's decision. Siddharth, do you want me to talk to them and get them to stop the transfer?"

Without looking at my boss, I paused, shook my head sideways and resumed crying.

Devyani rushed to my side and handed me a glass of water and a tissue paper. Wiping my tears, I looked at her in the eye like a lost puppy and started crying again.

"This is so not fair," cried out Navin. "When I cry, Di calls me a sissy, but when Siddharth does the same thing, he gets a glass of water!"

"Shut up, Navin," Devyani reprimanded Navin.

"What's wrong with him? Is he missing his parents or something?" asked my boss in a highly concerned tone to Amit.

"No sir, I think he is just drunk. May be he might be undergoing some hormonal changes in his body, who knows? I will take him home."

The note was no longer of any use. I took it out of my pocket, crumpled it and threw it out, before leaving.

●

A week later, I was at my neighbourhood auto stand, nursing a broken heart. The logistic plan was to take an auto up to Indore bus stand, and thereafter take an overnighter to Jabalpur. Amit and Navin had accompanied me to see me off. I was keen to get away from Indore at the earliest, once and for all.

There were two autos parked at the stand. I approached the first autowallah, who resembled a small time hoodlum in uniform. He didn't seem too excited on getting a customer.

"Indore bus stand?"

The fellow looked at me nonchalantly and declared coolly, "Five hundred rupees."

"Five hundred bucks? I am asking the fare from here to Indore bus stand, not the price of your entire auto. I will pay by the meter, nothing more or less."

"Meter is not working."

"Listen mister, don't think I am an outsider just because I look like one."

"Yeah, yeah. Five hundred bucks or take another auto."

Irked to the core, I approached the second autowallah, an elderly gentleman and seemingly more approachable.

"Indore bus stand?"

The veteran didn't even bother to look up from his newspaper. "Take the first auto. You can't break the queue."

I looked around, but there was no other transport in sight. I sighed and began to place my luggage in the first auto.

"Fifty rupees extra for the luggage," announced the hoodlum with a smirk. I had little choice but to give in to the extortion.

I looked in every direction with the hope of getting one final glimpse of Devyani. But there was no sign of her; I would have to be content with just her memories.

As I prepared to sit in the auto, Amit extended his hand for a handshake and said, "Take care, buddy. It was fun working together." I was thankful that he didn't broach the Devyani chapter.

I looked at Navin. With a sad look, Navin walked up to me, hugged me warmly and said, "I will miss you." *At least somebody would.*

Taking the cue from Navin, Amit lunged forward to give me a hug but stopped midway. "Oh look, we have company."

I looked up and saw a familiar figure running across the road in my direction. My heart skipped several beats. It was Devyani! *Hope at the end of the long dark tunnel.*

It was difficult for me to guess what Devyani was thinking, as she was panting heavily with all that sprinting. She asked Amit and Navin to leave us alone for a few moments. My heart was pounding rapidly.

I wiped my eyes and looked at Devyani. Dressed in simple, sleeveless white cotton salwar kameez, embroidered with the famous *Lucknowi chikan* artwork, Devyani had rarely looked more beautiful.

Devyani put a hand on my shoulder and asked in a concerned tone, "Are you all right?"

I sniffed and lied, "Yes. I am just recovering from a cold, that's all."

"Oh okay. I came here because I had to give you something and also talk to you."

"Give me what?" I asked with eager anticipation.

Devyani opened her purse and extracted a bulging brown wallet, which I recognized immediately.

"You had forgotten it in the office."

"That's it? You came here just to return my wallet?"

"No, I also wanted to tell you that I got your note. Actually, our maid found it while cleaning the house. Thank god, she didn't realize what it was, and gave it to me. Had she given it to mom or dad, it would have been a catastrophe. Why didn't you give the note to me directly?"

"I, I, er, tried many times but you were very passionate about your moong dal halva and I didn't want to break your flow. Did you... uh... read the note?"

"To be honest, it was quite difficult to understand the handwriting. And, there were so many cancellation marks! But after multiple attempts, I did get the broad idea. I never realized you had feelings for me, always looked upon you as a—"

"Please don't say brother."

"I was about to say friend, actually."

"That's even worse! What do you feel about me now?"

"You are a good person, Siddharth." I had a sinking feeling.

"You didn't answer my question."

"Siddharth, I really like you. But the fact is you barely know me."

"What is there to know? You are such a lovely, kind person. You have all the traits that I would want in my ideal life partner. The moment I met you, I knew you were my soulmate."

"*Whoa*, don't get all cheesy on me. You claim to know me? Okay, let me ask you a few questions."

"Try me."

"Which is my favourite flower?"

"Rose?" I answered apprehensively.

"I hate flowers."

"That was a trick question. Can you ask me another one, please?"

"Okay, which is my favourite drink?"

"Tea?"

"Wrong again. It is Tequila. Are you aware that I hold the record in my class for downing ten shots in one go?"

"That was a tough one! I am more of a tea drinker but am open to experimenting with Tequila, if you want."

"You think I am lovely and all? I don't think you would be ever able to handle my temper, mood swings or tantrums."

"Of course, I could. I am a very understanding—."

"You remember the time when our car was all bashed up?"

"Yes, I remember that. You had a close shave—

"Close shave, my foot. I was the one who crashed the car on purpose. I was mad at my ex boyfriend and vented my frustration on our car.

"Huh? Boyfriend?"

"*Ex*-boyfriend. And why are you looking so shell shocked? You thought that I couldn't have a boyfriend, eh?"

This was another trick question and I was not falling for it. "I... uhhmmm..."

"Are you going to take long? Waiting charges will be extra." The autowallah interrupted; he was beginning to lose patience.

"Hey mister, can't you see we are talking? Please shut up and wait." Devyani reprimanded him. This was a new side to Devyani that I had never witnessed.

Devyani turned her focus back on me. "You know how many affairs I have had?"

"Er, no. But I am guessing that you will tell me anyway."

"Four! All serious ones too."

Four? And I wasn't even in the consideration set! Oh lord, hope she didn't get physical or anything.

"That's okay. It's not like you had any…ahem… physical relationships or something. Not that it is any of my business."

"Why? Does it bother you that I could have a physical relationship?"

"Of course not. I am quite open-minded. That's your past; it's your present that decides your future." I put on a brave front and added in a lighter tone, "If it's any consolation, I have not had a single affair. Haha."

Devyani facial muscles tightened instead of relaxing. "You mean to say that you have zero experience?"

I took offence. "I am not a baby. I may have watched, you know, a little porn here and there. I know what happens."

Devyani rolled her eyes and exclaimed, "Unbelievable."

There were a few moments of uncomfortable silence. Finally it was Devyani who spoke up.

"Is that water in your eyes? Are you about to cry again, Siddharth?"

"Of course not! I have had an eye infection for some time now. And what do you mean by 'again'? I don't appreciate the insinuation." I sniffed.

Bloody stubborn tears! Wrong place, wrong time, always.

"Oh, okay. If you say so. It's that I can't handle grown men crying."

"Marry me, Devyani. Please," I literally begged. I was drowning; there was no time for subtlety.

"Siddharth, Siddharth, Siddharth," Devyani sighed and continued "You haven't listened to anything I have said so far, have you?"

"All you have done so far is to try and discourage me. But my determination remains strong as ever. I have learnt in life, never to give up. Whatever you have revealed to me about yourself has attracted me even more towards you. I love you."

"Listen pal, we are two very different people. I am already betrothed to someone and our families are involved. Don't make this difficult for both of us. I am sure you will make some lucky girl happy some day."

"But I don't want some girl. I want you. I miss you, Devyani. Why don't we make each other lucky?"

"Being the more 'experienced' person here, let me give you some advice. I don't know any other way of breaking this to you, but you are *not* in love with me. You are in love with the *image of me* that you have created in your brain by conveniently filling in the blanks. You have created my avatar in your head. Unfortunately, I am not that person. So, when you come to know the real me, there will be a gap between your expectation and reality, which will lead to disappointment. There is a second, more important reason – I don't love you."

I stood there, shell shocked.

"But you did say that you liked me?"

"Yes, but liking is not the same as loving. There is a big difference."

I was not throwing in the towel yet.

"But people learn to love also. Look at so many successful arranged marriages."

"Hmmm. You must get into the auto, you are getting late,"

"Please don't change topics. To hell with the auto! First, answer my question."

Devyani came close to me, grasped my shoulders and gave me a warm peck on my right cheek. Instinctively, I wanted to hug her tightly and kiss her on her lips, but all I could do was stand like a statue.

"Goodbye, Siddharth. You will understand someday, hopefully."

The *damn* tears flooded my eyes again as I tried to reckon with the hopelessness of situation. The impatient autowallah pressed the ignition switch of his auto and rotated the accelerator handle violently to make a point. I had lost all motivation, as I turned my back to Devyani, and boarded the auto mechanically. The auto picked up speed as the autowallah released his foot from the brake.

"Siddharth!" Devyani shouted.

I jutted my head out of the auto and swung around. Devyani was jogging to keep pace with the moving auto. I tapped the autowallah on his shoulder and pleaded, "Arrey, please stop this auto."

The rascal applied the brake so viciously that I was hurled forward, embracing the autowallah from behind, to avoid crashing into the windshield.

I got out of the auto. Devyani was smiling affectionately. Perhaps, my story was going to have a happy ending after all.

Devyani took out an envelope from her purse and gave it to me. The envelope had a base design in golden floral motifs with an embossed image of Lord Ganesh at the centre. Devyani took hold my right hand and caressed it gently.

"The 23rd of January. Please don't forget. I want to see you there. Have a safe and enjoyable trip."

It's not about *Dal Chawal*

"Hi baby, have you reached the hotel?"

It was the seventh time that Adhira, my live-in partner, had called me on my way from Jabalpur railway station to Refresh Residency Hotel.

"Yes sweetie, I have just reached. "

"I wish I was there with you."

"Sweetie, you know that I couldn't have taken you with me. This is an official trip. Besides, I am here for only two days."

"I know, but is there any problem in wishing? Two days is sooo long! Do you miss me, baby?"

"Not now, sweetie." Realising my blunder, I added hastily, "I mean yes, I miss you and all that. But it's just that I am a little hassled right now."

I just had a huge row with the cabbie over the 'miscellaneous' charges over and above the 'fixed' fare. And now, I had to heave two huge suitcases into the hotel lobby all by myself, while the hotel attendant remained conspicuously absent.

"Why, what happened baby? Are you all right?" There was palpable concern in Adhira's voice.

"Yes, yes, sweetie. Don't worry, I have everything under control. In fact, I am just checking in right now."

The hotel had a large atrium with beautiful red Japanese maple bonsai trees landscaping the wooden flooring. Artefacts from different states of India were placed in artificial crevices made in the walls and lit up with recessed LED lights. As I sauntered towards the lobby desk, a guy attired in a suit and tie walked up to me and gave me a plastic smile.

"How may I help you sir?"

"Maybe you can start by giving me a room?"

"Can I see your ID, sir?"

"Of course you can. But can you please ask someone to help me with my luggage?"

"Most certainly, sir."

Despite the assurance, no one came forth. I handed over my identity card to the fellow.

The fellow looked at the ID card and then at me, flashing his infuriating plastic smile again.

"You are Mr Mahir Adwait, right sir?"

"No, actually I am the Dalai Lama in disguise."

The guy looked confused for a couple of seconds and then began to bray loudly. "Hahaha…Nice joke, sir, nice joke."

My patience was running thin. "Look, are you going to give me a room or not?"

"I will take a copy of this ID. Can you fill this form out in the meantime?" the guy asked, handing me over a form that looked scary and exhaustive.

"Er, can I just sign here? You can fill in the remaining details."

"Sorry sir, but we are a little short on staff today. I am already multi-tasking, so I will have to request you to fill in the details yourself. Please do not leave any blank unfilled. I apologize for the inconvenience."

"What the &^%$#@!"

"Hello, hello… are you there, baby? Hello, hello?" It was Adhira again. I had forgotten to disconnect the call.

I placed the mobile on my ear again. "Yes, sweetie, I am—"

"Have you completed your check-in? How's the hotel?"

"Sweetie, give me a few minutes, I will call you back." This time, I made doubly sure to disconnect the call.

I finally managed to complete the form and handed it over to the reception manager. He checked his computer and looked at me sorrowfully.

"So sorry sir, we are sold out today."

"But that is not possible. I had made prior reservation with what's his name? Yes, Steven something."

"Sorry sir. But Steven no longer works for us. As I am checking in my computer, I can't see your name here."

I lost my fuse. "You take my ID, make me fill a huge form and now you say you can't give me a room? It's late and I am hungry and exhausted. Listen buster, I am not moving from here until I get a room."

"Okay sir, relax. Let me check again. Maybe I can work something out. As I can see now, we can arrange a makeshift room for you, but you need to pay a little extra."

"How much?"

"Not much sir. Only Rs 4000."

I gasped. "But the room tariff itself is Rs 2000. You are charging me double. That's outright extortion."

"No sir, this is called dynamic pricing. It's automatically done by the software; we have no control. Shall I make the booking, sir? We cannot hold on to the room for too long."

I resigned myself to the situation. "Okay, do it."

My cellphone was ringing, Adhira's name was flashing again.

"Hi baby, you forgot to call me? I was waiting so long for your call. You always say few minutes and then take hours to call back."

"Sorry sweetie…I didn't forget. I told you I will call back in a few minutes."

I looked at my watch; it had barely been ten minutes since we last spoke.

"Sorry, sweetie. It's just that I am completing my check in now."

"How's the room?"

"I don't know yet, I am waiting for them to allot me a room."

"Okay. Did you have your dinner?"

"Not yet."

"Why don't you have your dinner till such time they give you the room?"

"Okay sweetie, that's a good idea."

"But be very careful about what you eat. Hotel food can be very oily. Ask the hotel fellows to wash the vegetables properly. You can never trust these guys."

I sighed. "Yes mom, I mean sweetie—"

"I miss you so much. Do you miss me too, baby?"

"Yes sweetie, I already told you before that I miss you. Can I call you back later?"

"Yes, of course."

I proceeded to the hotel restaurant while they prepared my room. The hotel had two restaurants, an indoor one on the ground floor near the swimming pool and a second one on the terrace, facing the sky. Considering it was a breezy, full moon night, I opted for the latter option. The ambience appeared to be warm and cozy, with diffused lighting effects in natural warm colours. The chairs and tables were made from cane furniture, blending with the ambience. The restaurant was practically empty, so it was not difficult to locate a vacant table. A couple of waiters crossed my table on more than one occasion, but failed to notice my raised hand. After fifteen minutes of patient waiting and admiring the stars and the moon in the sky, I stood up and blocked a waiter's path.

"Excuse me, is someone going to take my order or not?"

"Of course sir. What would you like to have?"

"Which dish can you serve immediately? I am famished."

"Sir, we are short on staff today. Anything that you order, will take at least half an hour."

"No, no, that's too long."

"Sir, would you like to try our Italian Mushroom Risotto? We can get it in two minutes."

I became suspicious. "How will you make this dish so quickly? Hope you are not giving me leftovers?"

"No sir, we would never do that. A customer had ordered this dish and cancelled it at the last minute."

"Okay, get it. I just hope that you guys make a decent risotto in Jabalpur."

"Don't worry sir; it's the chef's specialty."

My phone began to ring yet again with Adhira's name flashing on the screen. I was not in a mood to talk but ignoring the call was not a good idea. I slid my finger on the phone screen to take the call.

"Hi baby. Did you have your dinner?"

"No sweetie, I've just ordered it. "

"You are not going to ask me what I had for dinner, baby?"

"Yes of course. What did you have for dinner, sweetie?"

"Nothing yet. I am trying out something special today which I want to feed you with my own hands when you get back."

"What?"

"I will tell you, first let me prepare it correctly. What have you ordered for dinner?

"I thought I'd try the Italian Mushroom risotto today. Feeling damn hungry."

There was a long pause at the other end. "Hello? Hello?"

"You always do this, don't you?" Adhira's voice had turned stony cold.

I was completely taken aback by the shift in mood. "Huh? What is the matter, sweetie?"

"You know that I am a foodie. Whenever we go out, I always say that we should try something different, but you always have bloody dal chawal. Two weeks ago when we went to Spice Kitchen, you said we will have dal chawal. Then when we went to the buffet dinner at Royal Feast, you said that you wanted only dal chawal. And I, like a fool, always listened to you."

My head was spinning in confusion. "I don't understand, sweetie. I have never tried to stop you from having whatever you wanted to eat."

"You will say that only, won't you? How do you think it would make me feel to gorge on Italian or Continental or Chinese while you have your dal chawal? I don't want to enjoy alone, I want you to enjoy with me. But no, you can't see beyond your damn dal chawal."

I tried to introduce some logic in the discussion. "But sweetie, I have never claimed to love hotel food. In fact, going out has always been your idea."

"So, now this is all my fault, is it?" Adhira's tone was increasing in pitch and volume. "Can't you ever look at things from other's perspective, for once?"

Hunger pangs had blocked my brain's ability to think beyond my stomach. I reacted instinctively, "I have no clue why are you making such a big deal about a non issue," irritation clearly apparent in my voice.

Ignoring my reaction, Adhira continued with her flow. "Now that you are alone, you decide to experiment with Italian and have fun all by yourself. Why didn't you have your dal chawal today also like other days?"

"I still don't understand, but if it makes you happy, I will cancel the order right now and order dal chawal."

"Don't you dare! Do whatever you feel like. I don't want to force you to do anything. I hate—"

The waiter re-appeared with a tray in his hand. "Sir, your delicious mushroom risotto is ready. Shall I serve it?" Alarmed, I put my index finger onto my lips, signaling to the waiter to shut up and take the tray back.

It was the waiter's turn to be confused now. "But sir," he began to protest.

I put covered the phone's microphone with my hand and growled at the waiter. "I told you to take the damn risotto back."

"But sir, we cannot cancel this dish two times. Who will have all this risotto?"

"I don't know. You have it. Or, throw it the dustbin, for all I care. I am having a very serious conversation right now."

I moved my hand away from the microphone. Adhira's diatribe was still on. "—You always try to tell me what to do, what not to do. Why does everything have to be your way?"

"Sweetie, you have a free will of your own. You always have a choice to—"

"Are you going to rub that in my face? Are you trying to play God by giving me a choice? "

"But I never said or even implied any such thing."

"There you go again. Why are you continuously arguing and defending yourself? Why can't you simply accept that you are wrong?"

I took a long breath and sighed. *I don't know why we are fighting. I have no idea which way this argument is going. I have zero idea how to end it. All I know that the longer this argument goes on, the more I stand to lose.*

In desperation, I pulled out my final card and said in a low voice. "I, uh…sweetie, I realize my mistake. I am sorry."

"Do you think that I am a puppy that you dole out a sorry and I will wag my tail? You can be so selfish!"

My last card had been discarded like a wet rag. I felt like pulling my hair out. "What do you really want to hear from me?"

"That is the basic problem. You never understand, you never *want* to understand."

There was silence in the background, followed by soft sobbing sounds. Adhira had played her trump card.

After what seemed like an eternal period of silence in ice age, I heard Adhira's voice again. "Do you care for me?"

"Yes, of course."

How much?

"A lot?"

"Not like that. You have to show me how much you care for me."

"Er, how do I show you over the phone?"

"I don't know. Use your imagination."

I racked my tired brain cells to come up with something appropriate.

I care for you as much as much as a chef cares for his food, a bird for his nest, a mechanic for his car, a doctor for his patient.

"Well? Are you going to show me or not?"

"Wait, wait, I am thinking."

"Can you jump off a tall building for me?"

"You know that I am scared of heights—"

"That's true. Okay, if I was drowning, would you jump into the water to save me?"

"But baby, I don't know how to swim. Besides, you are an expert swimmer. Why do you need me to save you?"

"True again. Okay, how about this? Would you walk over a bed of coals for me?"

"Hot or cold?"

"Hot, of course."

"Sure I could do that, especially with the latest flame retardant material they have these days—"

"Why do you have to be so logical, so practical? Can't you be romantic for once?"

"I am so sorry, sweetie."

"Say it a hundred times."

Left with little choice, I apologized a hundred times and regained my peace.

No sooner had I disconnected the call, I ran to the kitchen. I spotted the waiter, but he was no longer in uniform.

"Do you have anything to eat? Anything at all?"

"Sir, the kitchen is closed. Nothing else will be available right now."

"What about the mushroom risotto?"

"Sir, we threw it out like you ordered."

I heard a pinging sound on my cellphone; it was a Facebook notification by Adhira. The post had received 981 likes; it had a picture of a beaming Adhira next to a copper pot filled with some kind of liquid.

The picture was captioned:

'Yay! My first successful attempt at *Dal Panchratna*. Loving it!'

Bossy Affair

The weekend

My phone kept ringing incessantly but I was resolute in not responding. I was not about to fritter away a hard earned weekend on professional exigencies. Each time 'Jackass' flashed on my smart phone screen, I would silence the ring tone by tapping the side button.

I opened the pages of my morning newspaper and resumed my leisure reading, when suddenly I heard a loud banging on my door.

"Hey baby, how long are you going to stay cooped in there?" It was Adhira, my live-in partner.

"Uh…give me ten minutes." *Thank god, my door was locked.*

"You said ten minutes half an hour ago. By the way, where is today's newspaper? Are you by any chance reading the newspaper sitting on the pot?"

"Er, I…" I hesitated replying.

"I have told you so many times not to read the newspaper in there. It's not good for your bowels. You should focus on your morning ablutions, not multi-task."

There you go again, showing off with big words. Can't you say 'potty' like normal people? Why don't you focus on your business please and leave me alone at this crucial juncture?

"I am not reading the newspaper, sweetie."

"Try not to wet the newspaper. And, can you hurry up please? I want to use the washroom too, it's an emergency."

"Sure sweetie, only five minutes more."

My cell phone started ringing again with 'Jackass' flittering on my screen.

"I don't believe it! You have your cell phone also with you, inside?"

"*Uh-huh.* I don't know how it came inside, honest." One of my chums had recently forwarded the latest edition of *Playboy* via WhatsApp; this was the only private place in the house wherein I could view the magazine safely.

As I hurriedly tried to silence the phone, I accidentally hit the answer button, to my horror. A demonic voice screamed out of the phone.

"Why are you not picking up your damn phone, Mahir? I have been calling you so many times. And where the hell are you right now?"

I had little choice left but to reply.

"Uh, good morning sir. I was about to call you sir. I—"

"Why are you whispering? I can barely hear you." The voice at the other end roared.

"Sir, I am at the doctor's."

"What are you doing at the doctor's?"

"I am suffering from fever and loose motions."

"You have fever and loose motions?"

"Yes sir."

"You young guys are so weak, falling sick every second day. I hope you are not planning to take sick leave, are you?"

"Sir, I didn't' want to and explicitly told the doctor that I can't afford to miss office. But the doctor said—"

"Nonsense, take some pills or injections and get a move on, for god's sake. By the way, what happened to the payment we were expecting from Ramanuj Associates? We are having a huge cash flow situation this month."

*I am having a flow situation myself, you arse****!*

"Sir, we will get the payment soon, I am on top of the situation. But there are a few hurdles, the Bill of Exchange—"

*Always better to keep some excuse cards in hand just in case of last minute f***** by Ramanuj. The company was more slithery than an oily soap.*

"Spare me the nitty gritty, will you? I want the payment in our account by the end of the week. Make sure of it, do you understand?"

Stress was beginning to build up rapidly inside me.

"Yes, sir."

"What is that strange whooshing sound on the phone?" I suddenly realized that I had unwittingly pressed the flush knob.

"Sir, it's a signal—"

"Never mind, give me a report every four hours on the progress, without fail."

"But sir," *Click.* The guy had already disconnected the call.

I was seething in rage. For a couple of moments, I toyed with the idea of throwing my phone into the commode. I would have done so, had it not been for the fact that it was a brand new, expensive, state of the art smartphone.

Newspaper and *Playboy* would have to wait. Ramanuj Associates was top priority now. My weekend was ruined. Thanks to the Jagmohan *M*&%@C$*^%B$#@C** Khurana, my boss!

I couldn't do it any longer, my intestines were jammed. I collected the phone and newspaper and stormed out of the WC, blood boiling, devising multiple ways to murder my boss.

"Hey, that was quick, for a change," remarked Adhira, who was sitting on the sofa with her laptop. "And why are you not wearing anything?"

Realization dawned upon me and I scampered back to the WC to get my towel, cursing Khurana under my breath.

Adhira entered the washroom even as I was exiting it. Putting on a huge smile, she instructed, "Baby, now that you have some free time today, can you do the vacuuming of the house?"

Before I could protest, the door was shut on my face.

As if one Khurana was not enough! My Sunday would now be dedicated to *&^%$#@*! Ramanuj Associates and *&^%%*! vacuum cleaner.

Just another day at work

"You look really stressed out, man. Chill yaar," Benoy Gupta remarked, as he handed over a cutting chai to me at the local roadside tea stall. Benoy worked in administration and was two years my junior.

"My life has become worse than that of a *&^%#@ street dog. This Khurana &^%$#@ is becoming unbearable every day. The &^%$#@ fellow works my butt off during the week and then ruins my weekend also. He thinks I am his personal slave. The *&^%$@ hasn't heard of the concepts of work life balance or respect for your colleagues. He gives me all the shitty jobs in office. Worst of all, there is no appreciation for any work that I do. It's a long dark tunnel with no light at the end.*^%$# **&^%!"

"Hmmm," Benoy muttered blandly.

I was in my flow. "Just today morning, I had another huge fight with that *@&^%%$!"

"What happened?"

"It's that Ramanuj Associates matter; can't seem to get the monkey off my back. Khurana gave the company goods on credit, and now, when they are not paying, he wants me to go and sit in front of the managing director's cabin until they pay up. What does he think I am? Did I do my engineering for this crap?"

"So what's the problem? Just go there and sit, na."

"Sure. But first I have to get entry to their office. What if the security guards don't allow me inside at all?"

"Hmmm."

"I told my boss today morning, that their managing director is travelling out of the country for a week."

"And?"

"A normal guy would have told me to defer my visit to Ramanuj by a week. But this psycho blasted me saying that I should have kept track of the managing director's schedule. And if he was not there, then I should go and sit in front of his secretary."

Benoy chuckled. "You could play some eye blinking games with the secretary."

"Arrey, don't you see? What is the sense in sitting next to the secretary and staring at her all day, hoping to recover our money? What if I got charged with sexual harassment?"

"Er, I think that's a remote possibility. Ramanuj Associates MD's secretary is a male."

"Whatever! I felt like pounding his head on his desk then and there."

"The secretary's?"

"You are not listening, Benoy. Khurana's."

"Can I tell you something, Mahir? You can't stay in the same river as the crocodile and fight with it. You are so unhappy in this job; why don't you start searching? I am sure there are so many opportunities out there for talented guys like you."

"Sahi yaar, you are right! I have been so engrossed with my job that this company is taking me for a ride. Loyalty is for the dogs.

If only I had an option or two in my hand! This company will only understand my value once I am gone."

"But why wait unnecessarily and subject yourself to more humiliation? My suggestion is that you consider putting in your papers and devote full time to finding a better opportunity more suited to your talent."

"Hmmmm."

"And look at the bright side. You can spend more time with your beautiful girlfriend. Anyway, Adhira is working, so she can help ease your temporary financial crunch."

"Yeah, yeah," I remarked wryly. My back was still hurting with all the vacuuming over the weekend, although I was amply rewarded for my efforts later by a very happy Adhira. But unlike Adhira, there were no side benefits with Khurana.

"Okay, that's it; I have made up my mind. Thanks a lot Benoy, for your great suggestion."

Benoy was taken by surprise. "Huh….you are going to put in your papers right now?"

"Of course not, that would be stupid. I am going to book my train ticket to Ramanuj Associates, Hyderabad, for tomorrow morning."

●

The Aggravation

"You didn't go to Hyderabad?" Benoy asked casually.

"That's it. I am done with Khurana!" My body quivering with rage, I almost spilt the *cutting chai* onto my new shirt.

"Hmmmm," Benoy acknowledged, sipping casually from his glass, unruffled by my extreme reaction. Disappointed at not getting a more sympathetic reaction from Benoy, I elaborated.

"You know what happened?" I took a deep breath. "Khurana asked me to apologize to the MD of Ramanuj Associates. Of all the &^%$#@&*!"

"But why didn't you go to Hyderabad?"

"Arrey, you are not listening again, Benoy. Try keeping up with me. I told you that I didn't get train tickets. So I decided to do the smart thing and call up the MD directly."

"And then?"

"It was only after repeated attempts that the MD picked up my call, only to warn me not to call again. I told him that it gave me no pleasure in calling him but I was under tremendous pressure from my management to recover the dues and that if Ramanuj did not pay up, I could even lose my job."

"What did he say?"

"He simply said that he didn't know me and didn't appreciate the tone of my voice before disconnecting the call. *Just like that!* And then an hour later, I get a call from Khurana, screaming at me."

"Why was Khurana screaming at you?"

"Apparently the *bastard* MD had complained to Khurana. According to the MD, I had disturbed him during his overseas trip and spoken to him very rudely. He also claimed that he had incurred heavy international roaming charges because of me. I am sure that *&^%$!* was lying through his teeth, he was in India only. I was so pissed off that I gave it back."

"To the MD?"

"Arrey no, you are not paying attention again. I gave it back to Khurana, K-H-U-R-A-N-A."

"Oh, okay this is all a little confusing. What did you tell Khurana exactly?"

"I told him bluntly that he was speaking too loudly and fast and that I couldn't understand what he was saying."

Benoy's face eyebrows arched inwards in disbelief. "How did he react?"

"There was a huge pause on the other side. I think the guy was speechless. I disconnected the call in irritation. Even as I speak now, my blood is boiling." I clenched my teeth and wrung my hands in opposite directions, imagination running wild. I spotted a random pebble lying on the street. I picked it up and threw it with all my might. The pebble flew for a few meters and struck an unoccupied sedan parked on the other side of the road, causing a small dent on the front door of the car.

"What was that sound?"

"What sound? I didn't hear anything. Let's get back to office quickly," I replied anxiously, wanting to make a quick getaway from the *chai tapri* before anyone noticed my little misdemeanor.

As we headed back to the office, Benoy announced, "Have you heard the latest? The promoters have announced that there will be an employee engagement survey conducted by Opinionated in our company."

"You mean it's some kind of employee satisfaction survey?"

"Kind of."

"Ha. I don't trust such surveys. Do you remember the Chinese fellow Mao, who did a similar survey with his party workers, got them to speak up and later on screwed their happiness?"

"Maybe, but this is not China. The interesting feature with the Opinionated survey is that while the consolidated feedback would be made public within Elixir, the actual feedback documents will be kept strictly confidential and not be shared with anyone at Elixir, including the promoters. It will be the perfect revenge platform for the trampled, exploited, overworked, abused worker."

"Which worker?"

"I was referring to you."

●

Leave request

Jagmohan Khurana's cabin was already open. A bald pate, islanded by straws of unevenly dispersed hair, moved from left to right like a mechanical typewriter. Khurana was busy studying a file. I knocked hesitatingly on the huge name plate affixed on the door titled, 'Jagmohan Khurana, General Manager'.

"Good afternoon, sir," I wished gingerly.

Khurana looked up at me and threw a puzzled look. "Did I call for you?"

"Sir, well, we were discussing Ramanuj Associates when the phone signal went bad and you couldn't hear me?" *At least that is what I hope had happened.*

"Ramanuj, Ramanuj, what were we discussing? Ah, yes, now I remember," Khurana mumbled in a flat tone before hollering out of the blue, "What is wrong with you? Have you totally lost your common sense? Why are you working like a donkey? Who authorized you to talk to the MD of Ramanuj Associates without my permission?"

"But sir, how else was I supposed to—"

"No, no, just answer my question. Who authorized you to talk to the MD? Did you even bother to check with me?"

"No sir. But sir—"

"Are you aware that the bugger made a threat to *my boss* Madhav Kriplani to cut off all future orders to our company if we pestered him in any way?"

"I am sorry to hear that sir, but you only—"

"Why didn't you inform me earlier?"

"But sir, how could I?"

"I had given you a simple instruction to go and sit in his office, not do anything silly. But what do you do? Firstly, you cancel your trip to Hyderabad of your own accord."

"But sir, train tickets were not——"

Khurana was in flow and would not be interrupted. "Secondly, you talk to the MD without my permission. Thirdly, you upset him by speaking to him rudely. And to top it all, you don't even bother to inform me about your conversation. One blunder after another——"

When Khurana had finished presenting his case, even I felt ashamed of myself. So I took an aggressive defensive stance.

"Sir, this MD fellow is one big liar. I had spoken to him very politely."

"Whom do you expect me to believe – you or him?"

"Me, of course."

"That was meant to be a rhetorical question, you duffer."

"Sir, if you take my opinion, do we really need customers like Ramanuj Associates? They have a bad market reputation, never pay on time and keep blackmailing us."

"That is beside the point. Anyway, I didn't ask you for your opinion. You know how embarrassing this episode has been for me in front of Madhav Kriplani? Anything that gets escalated is an indirect slap on my face. And make that two slaps on yours. Rather, make that three."

I tried to protest vehemently, "But sir, I never wanted to do this. This entire idea of pursuing the MD was——"

"Mahir, please take responsibility for your actions and stop blaming others. Look at me! Do you ever hear me griping about Madhav Kriplani, even though the whole world says he is an *idiot*? No, never."

"Actually sir, I can remember at least three instances in the last one month wherein——"

"*Silence!* Do you know that you have an attitude problem? Unless you do some self-introspection and improve, it is very difficult for us to work together. I am already regretting my decision to put you in charge of the Ramanuj Associates account. Listen, we have to do some damage control before this issue spirals out of control. Prepare an apology note draft for the MD and a separate failure report for Madhav Kriplani; show it to me by today evening."

"But sir, why should I apologize?"

"Don't argue, just do it."

"Nike."

"What did you say?"

"Nothing sir." *Enough of Ramanuj *&^%$.* I desperately needed a break, run away from everything and get back a semblance of control. Besides, Adhira had been nagging me for a holiday to Shimla for quite some time now. I had to be firm and assertive with my request with Khurana.

"Sir, err, I know this is not a good time. But, I, uh, ahem wanted to request you for something."

Khurana looked at me suspiciously. "Hope you are not going to ask me for leave, are you? You are taking a lot of holidays nowadays."

Damn! I had to think on my feet.

"But sir, the last time you had given me leave was exactly a year and half ago. I have been working so hard and—"

"So? Where are the results? All our projects are running late, our collections are poor and you want to take leave now? I don't believe it."

I am trying my best, don't have a magic wand.

This discussion was not going anywhere; I pulled out the ace in my sleeve. "Sir, I had planned to take a religious pilgrimage."

It would not be a lie if I could identify a couple of important temples in Shimla for paying a customary visit.

I prayed that Khurana would not ask me the destination.

"Where had you planned to go?" A surprised Khurana quizzed me.

Double damn!

"Err, Tirupati."

Khurana's tone softened noticeably. "Hmmm. I don't want to come in the way of your spiritual obligations, but it will be difficult to explain your absence to Madhav Kriplani at such a sensitive time. I will defend you the best I can, but one cannot predict Madhav. Who knows how he might react? You know what I am hinting at, don't you?"

"But sir—"

"Madhav could very well say that if Mahir can't handle the responsibility, give it to someone else. I wouldn't want that to happen. If I were in your place, I would cancel the trip. First, resolve the Ramanuj Associates mess and then go."

It was the performance of a master manipulator, playing out the classic good cop, bad cop routine.

I had to think on my feet. "But sir, all the arrangements like flight tickets and hotel accommodation have already been made. I will not get a refund. In addition, my holidays will lapse if I don't utilize them in this calendar year." It was not the smartest thing to say under the circumstances, but then, I was desperate.

Khurana pondered for a few seconds before replying with a forced smile. "I can't force you to do anything against your will. The Opinionated employee survey is coming up and you should not have any ill feeling towards me, not that I care for any such survey. After all, we are working on the same team, aren't we? Forget all the rough words that I may have told you earlier, it was all in a fatherly manner. But it would help if I could see the apology note draft and the failure report by today evening, considering appraisals are next month. I am not linking the two, just reminding you, that's all."

Opinionated survey! I had completely forgotten about it. My one chance to salvage the situation. I would pretend to put in my papers and scare Khurana into granting me the leave.

"Sir, I have to make a confession."

'Sure, my boy. Go ahead, you have nothing to worry about."

"Sir, Adhira has been complaining a lot about the lack of work life balance. Please don't misunderstand me, I don't mind it at all because I respect your leadership and love this job. But Adhira simply refuses to understand, she complains about me being a workaholic. It is to pacify her that I promised to take her to Tirupati. "

Khurana looked puzzled. "Who is this Adhira?"

"She is my… uh… girlfriend."

Khurana puzzlement increased. "You have a girlfriend? Why don't you get married like others? Only have fun and no responsibilities. So typical of your generation."

How about minding your own business, generation B.C.?

Dodging the question, I brought back focus to the discussion. "Then there is the Opinionated survey."

There was a look of alarm on Khurana's face. "What about the Opinionated survey?"

"I understand that the survey will be held within this month. I could come back from my leave and fill up the survey. Not that I am trying to link my leave and the survey in any way." I paused for effect before adding dramatically to help Khurana make up his mind. "Adhira has even given me an ultimatum to leave me if I don't get the leave. I know it sounds silly and childish, but you know how women can be some times."

"Hmmm." Khurana drummed his fat fingers on the table and seemed immersed in thought. After a couple of minutes, he looked at me softly and remarked, "Okay."

Were my ears playing tricks on me?

"Does this mean that my leave is approved?"

"No, the okay means that I have heard you out. So you have problems at home. Big deal, who doesn't? Grow up, deal with it. I will think about your leave. Now get back to work."

There was no sense in debating a lost cause further with an irrational person. As I walked out of the cabin, crestfallen, I heard Khurana's voice trailing me.

"Make sure to send the apology note draft and the failure report by today evening."

The good news

I opened the door wearily. An ebullient Adhira flew into my limp arms, hugging me tightly. "Hi baby, you are back home early today! How was your day?"

Wriggling free from Adhira's grasp, I shut the door and replied, "Not so great. I had a fight with my boss."

Adhira's forhead shriveled with alarm, making her worry lines visible.

"Again? Hope you didn't do anything rash and impulsive, baby?"

"You don't have to patronize me. I am not a child," I replied, irritated.

"Of course, baby. It's just that I am concerned. I don't want you to repeat past mistakes of taking a spur of the moment decision, only to repent later. You have to remember that any decision that you take affects both of us."

"Yeah yeah," I grunted unhappily.

"Did you get your leave sanctioned from your boss? We need to book the train tickets and the hotel rooms *asap*."

"Not yet. But I am trying my best."

"You need to try harder, baby. I know you have a difficult boss, but if you really want something, you can get it done."

Always ready with gyan. Adhira was generally sweet, but sometimes she could be so full of it. "Can I suggest something?"

I wanted to say *No, I am not in the mood,* but Adhira had already started. "Why don't you try to have a one on one conversation with your boss? Ask him why he always picks on you and gives you such a hard time. Share your problems and concerns with him. Also try to see things from his perspective. Make a list of his positives and focus on them. I am sure things will improve between the two of you."

Yak, yak, yakity yak. First you work with Khurana and only then talk.

I avoided eye contact and replied tamely, "Yes sweetie."

Adhira hugged me again and whispered, "Won't you ask me about my day, baby? I have something special to tell you. Guess what?"

I froze with terror, she had *the look* on her face. I swallowed and croaked. "You are not pregnant, are you?" I cursed myself for not using protection for one solitary day in the previous month, when all the medical stores had gone on strike.

Adhira slapped my shoulders playfully and remarked, "No, no baby. Guess again."

Phew, that was a close shave.

"Sweetie, you know I am not very good at all these guessing games. Why don't you tell me directly?"

"I got my promotion today with a 15% hike in salary," Adhira declared jubilantly.

"*Again?* That's two times in two years already." I bit my tongue immediately; it was not the most appropriate response.

"Can you believe it? And the best part is that I didn't even ask for it this time."

Of course, I couldn't believe it. This was a monumental assault on my ego and self-confidence. Here I was, unable to even get a leave sanction from my boss. I did the mental math. A 15% hike on an already inflated salary meant that I could never hope to catch up with Adhira's pay package, working at Elixir Solutions. *Not in this lifetime at least.*

I gave a clumsy peck on Adhira's cheek. "Congratulations."

"Let's go out and celebrate tonight, baby."

"Sweetie, I am not feeling too well right now. Besides, I need to do make some job applications tonight."

"Hmmm. How's your job search coming along?"

"I have posted my resume on some of the mainstream online job search agencies. As a matter of fact, one of them called me up to say that they were very impressed with my CV and went on to offer me a discounted package deal to improve my resume, using advanced analytics. They will circulate it to over 5000 recruitment agencies. "

"You said no, right?"

"Of course, I accepted. It was a once in a lifetime offer."

"How much did they charge you?"

"Only three grand." *The actual figure was thirty grand, payable in ten instalments but I didn't want to bore Adhira with minor details.*

"Have you received any interview calls yet?"

"Not yet, but I expect they should start flowing soon. I have already received over a dozen calls with the guys, explaining the prospective job roles to me, noting down my interest and promising to revert soon. But I have to be choosy, can't make everyone happy."

"That's great, baby."

"Yeah. I am also super excited about this overseas placement consultant who has promised to get me a job in prestigious companies in Europe, USA and Australia. The agency lady assured me that my salary package would be fantastic, good enough for both of us to lead a lavish lifestyle."

"But baby, why overseas? I am happy being in India and don't want to leave my job. Hope that consultant has not asked for any fee?"

"She has asked for one time registration fee of Rs 2000 for running necessary background checks on my immigration record. They will refund this fee, if I don't pass the checks." *This was not a good time to mention that I had already paid the registration fee of Rs 5000 to the consultant.*

"Baby, thank goodness you have not paid this so-called consultant. These consultant types are frauds who target simpletons and then before you know it, they have gobbled up your money. Not that you are a simpleton, baby."

I had a sinking feeling in my stomach.

"What about that recruitment agency contact that you got from that office fellow, Benoy?"

"Benoy is not just any fellow. He is a good friend, sweetie."

"Whatever. Somehow, I have never liked that character! But no harm in meeting his contact."

"Aah, you mean Ritwik Ghoshal. Benoy talks very highly about him. I have spoken to Ritwik. He has given me an appointment next week."

"Appointment? You have got to be kidding me."

"No sweetie, he is a very busy man. He didn't want to meet me initially, but relented after I took Benoy's name."

"Okay baby, if you say so."

"Enough talk about me now. It's your day today. Let us have a candle light dinner at home."

"*Oooh,* that's so romantic! Are you going to cook something special?"

"Wait a minute, I thought that after one week of cooking on the trot, you would be taking over from me today?" Looking at Adhira's rapidly changing expression, I added hurriedly, "No sweat, I will make my signature dish today."

"I would love that, baby. What is your signature dish, by the way?"

"It's cheese omelette with Maggi noodles, sprinkled with oregano powder and tomato ketchup. It will be my first time today."

The worry lines on Adhira's forehead became visible again. "*Ahem*, baby, honey, please don't take this otherwise, but I think it's best if we order food from outside today. I will get the candles."

●

Opinionated survey

Khurana was speaking in an alien language. "My dear boys and girls, it gives me great joy to address this great team of ours. It is a very emotional day for me today. I may not have said this earlier, but I want to tell you now that I have always considered each one of you seated here as my own son and daughter."

We were looking at each other with blank faces, wondering what the hell was going on. So were the two coordinators from Opinionated, who were seated right beside me; they looked exasperated.

"Who allowed this idiot to speak? Did you forget the instructions?" The senior coordinator whispered to his harried junior.

"I don't know sir. This fellow forcibly entered the room and started talking on his own."

Khurana continued, unabated. "Surveys will come and go, but remember to be true to all those who are close to you, true to all those who have stood with you in difficult times, true to those who have taught you and helped you grow.

"So, I want to encourage each one of you to give your frank opinion and not be influenced by anyone."

The senior coordinator had just about enough. He stood up and told Khurana in a terse voice. "Sir, this is a confidential survey. You will need to leave the room."

Khurana was unfazed. "Yes, yes. I am just giving my team some moral support. Just one minute more, I am almost done. Like I was saying, boys and girls, if you need me, you know where to find me. I am always there for you."

Both the coordinators were standing up now, on the verge of pushing Khurana out of the room. "Sir, please leave, *now*."

"Okay, if you really insist."

"Sir, we really insist."

Once Khurana had left, the senior coordinator locked the door and began to read out the instructions while his junior distributed the survey sheets.

"We are conducting this survey within Elixir at multiple locations, simultaneously. There are eight subjective questions. Keep your replies brief and precise, preferably not more than three to four lines. We will use technology to gauge the employee engagement sentiment from your replies. Do not forget to put your name and employee code on the top right hand corner of the sheet. Remember that individual feedback will remain absolutely confidential, it will not be shared with anybody. Hence, give your opinion, freely and frankly, without fear."

There were so many ifs and buts whizzing around in my head. *What was the guarantee that the survey documents would not fall in the wrong hands? Khurana's little soliloquy was not a good omen. On the other hand, this might be the one opportunity for me to score a goal against my boss. I couldn't just fritter away the opportunity. Oh man, why was life so complicated?*

I started reading the questions as soon as the form was given. The questions looked deceptively simple. *What are the other implications/ connotations/ hidden messages?* My mind went blank; I had to read the questions multiple times before I was able to eke out the answers.

Q1: Do you know what is expected from you at work?
'Alexander Pope once said that blessed is he who expects nothing, for he shall never be disappointed. But to specially answer the question, I am generally expected to do the impossible. This is okay with me as another wise guy said — Nothing is impossible.'

Q2: Does your company provide you with all the tools and equipment to get the job done?

'Resourcefulness is the art of getting the job done with the least possible. Other than this, no comments.'

Q3: In the last one month, have you received recognition for your work?

'The question is not clear to me. Depends upon what one defines as recognition. Also, does this mean public or private recognition?'

Q4: Does your supervisor care about you and encourage your development?

'My supervisor has helped me appreciate the good in other people and made me a better human being. I know he cares about me because whenever I am not in office, he misses me.'

Q5: Does your supervisor respect your opinions?

'I would like to think so, but cannot say for sure, because he has never asked for them.'

Q6: How has been your experience working with Elixir Solutions?

'I consider myself honored to have worked with esteemed colleagues and superiors from whom I have learnt so much. I would like to take this opportunity to especially thank my boss, Mr Jagmohan Khurana, a leader exemplar, for the reasons listed below:

    a.   *Mr Khurana has taught us to pursue our professional dreams, nullify the concept of personal space / life and devote ourselves wholeheartedly into achieving our superior's aims and aspirations and by inference, the organizational goals. Being a practical leader, he has showed me that the theoretical concept of work life balance is just that – theoretical.*

    b.   *Mr Khurana treats me like a member of his own family. He often asks me to drive around his family and also run personal* errands like buying groceries or paying electricity bills.

c. *Mr Khurana has taught me generosity and the concept of giving. Whenever we go on joint tours, he ensures that I foot the bills even though his allowance is ten times that of mine. Although the learning has been painful, the process has developed my patience and record keeping capability.*

To be continued *

At this juncture, I had to perforce request for an extra blank answer sheet, to the astonishment of my colleagues and the Opinionated coordinators. The junior coordinator apologized saying that there was no blank A4 sheet available in the room, as no one had ever envisioned the need for it. But he tore off a page from his note book and handed it to me, which I accepted gratefully. Ignoring the amused looks in my direction, I continued writing.

* *continued from previous page*

d. *Mr Khurana has taught me (and many of my other colleagues) punctuality and the powers of observation. Tactically positioning his cabin near the entrance, he keeps an eye on all those coming late and never fails to point it out to defaulters. He has also taught us that our job is not a typical 9 to 5 one and the benefits of late sitting. Mr Khurana conducts many important impromptu meetings after 6 p.m. giving valuable inputs and leadership guidance to all those present. I would like to digress here a little stating that Mr Khurana has always discouraged us from having fast food, even when we are hungry. During many of such late night meetings, he often orders for coffee, pizza, coke, cashew nut biscuits, and chips, but takes special care never to offer such food to us. This has also helped us increase our tolerance for hunger.*

e. *Mr Khurana is a true motivator. He pulls down my pants in public whenever I make a mistake so that I (along with others) can learn from my mistake and avoid repeating it. Whenever I do well (which is an extremely rare phenomenon), Mr Khurana praises me privately. Mr Khurana has won the best manager's award a few times now; this is not surprising.*

f. *Mr Khurana has taught me to embrace work which has no relation to my educational qualifications, widening my professional horizons.*

g. *Mr Khurana has taught me the value of thriftiness by forcing me to travel to customer locations vide sleeper class train or state transport buses, even though I am eligible for air travel. Mr Khurana always tells me, 'Only if each one of us makes a small sacrifice, only then we can build this company, this country.' Mr Khurana would never fly business class himself had it not been for health reasons (of which I am unaware).*

h. *Mr Khurana promotes conflict between peers – says that it keeps us mentally fit and that it is better for the organization.*

i. *Like all great people have their share of critics / detractors, alas Mr Khurana has also not been spared. Just because the attrition rate in this company is one of the highest in the industry at a staggering 30% per year, that doesn't make Mr Khurana a bad boss. This propaganda is the work of our competitors. What people outside the company don't know is that all these people have not left; they have been sacked for incompetence. At least two employees are sacked every day. So where is the question of attrition? Mr Khurana has done all these people a favour.*

The list of virtues is never ending.

PS: I know I have exceeded four lines in the last question, but I couldn't control myself. I am sorry about the same.'

Q7: If you were to change anything at Elixir, what would it be?
'Maybe I would change a few lightings, add a few fans, shift the furniture, redo the painting, etc. Yes, I almost forgot, I would like to change the office canteen contractor.'

Q8: Would you recommend Elixir to other people?
'Is this a trick question? No comments.'

The room was already empty (except for the two Opinionated coordinators) by the time I had finished and submitted my filled up form.

Survey aftermath

Adhira's promotion had created an upheaval inside me; I had lost all sleep. I *had* to get my own promotion and increment and reclaim my sense of self-worth. I barged into Khurana's cabin without permission, but slowed down on sensing the somber mood inside. Khurana was sitting on his chair, pressing his temples with his fingers intermittently. He looked extremely unhappy.

I bent forward and asked haltingly. "Sir, could I?"

Khurana opened his eyes and barked, "Not now, I have a splitting headache."

"Sir, maybe this is not a good time. But could I get just a few minutes of your valuable time?"

Khurana tore open a drug strip, took out a white pill and popped it into his mouth. "I have already told you Mahir, I will think about your leave and revert. I have more important things to think about right now."

"Sir, actually, it was not about the leave."

"Then what?"

"It's just that I joined Elixir four years ago as a junior engineer. I have always tried to do my best. India's GDP is growing at 7% but inflation has kept pace with GDP growth rate. There is a demand in the market for experienced people—"

"I can't make out head or tail of what you are saying. If you have a point, make it quick."

"Sir, what I want to say is that even after spending four years of my most productive life for Elixir, I am still a junior engineer with the same salary as four years ago. So if we look in real terms, considering inflation, my salary has actually reduced."

"So?"

"Sir, I was hoping that I uh—" The words were just not coming out of my mouth.

"Speak out, for god's sake."

"—to get a promotion and increment this year."

"*What?*" Khurana roared. "How can you even think of a promotion at a time like this?"

I felt ashamed of myself.

"First you people betray me and stab me in the back. Now you want a promotion?"

I became anxious. "Why sir, what did I do?"

"I have just received the survey results from Opinionated."

"*Ohh*! Didn't realize that the feedback is unfavourable."

"No! It's all very confidential, but I can secretly share with you that the feedback has been excellent. Madhav Kriplani called up personally to congratulate me. There are a few grey areas here and there, which need to be ironed out. Have to take the bad with the good, that's leadership."

I feigned ecstasy and asked, "So I take it that all is well then?"

"No, we have some traitors in our midst who exploited my munificence. And why are you giving me that blank look?"

"Sir, what does munificence mean?"

"*Sheesh*, I am dealing with a bunch of back-stabbing, ignorant philistines. Tell me the truth, Mahir; did you write any crap about me in that survey?"

My body stiffened, I shook my head sideways vigorously in denial. "*Absolutely not* sir. I cannot even imagine anything bad about you, forget about writing something. If only there was some way I could show you some of my survey replies, you would have been proud of me."

"Unfortunately, these Opinionated guys didn't share the documents. Instead, they gave me a long lecture about integrity and ethics and all that crap."

Thank god!

"I take your word for it, but I still want you to find out the quislings in our team. I can only trust you."

I didn't know the meaning of quislings either, but didn't want to ask Khurana again. "Sir, ahem, could you think about my promotion now? I really need it."

"There you go again, just when I was starting to build a positive image about you. A promotion is given to those who deserve it, my boy, not those who need it."

"Okay sir, I correct myself. I deserve the promotion."

"Haven't you learnt anything from my experience? Climbing the corporate ladder is fraught with all kinds of dangers. Jealousy, politics, difficult subordinates and then surveys like Opinionated. Is it really worth the trouble?"

"Sir, I am willing to rise up to the challenge if you give me the opportunity."

Khurana let out a long sigh. "One problem at a time. First, we have to find a solution to your leave."

Khurana was again ducking the issue. My blood shot up to my brain cells. I lost composure and flared up.

"Sir, I wanted to tell you that I have been receiving offers from a number of companies. But I have been saying no to them in the hope of getting a promotion this year."

"Are you making a threat?" Khurana asked in a menacing tone.

I sensed danger signals and calmed down right away. "Never sir, I wouldn't dream of it. It's just that I have worked for four years under your leadership and I need to show some progress. It would be unfair to your leadership, if I stagnated. I don't want the company to lose out on a valuable resource after investing in me."

"Hmmm. What is the guarantee that you will continue with Elixir after you are promoted?"

I was foxed. "Sir, I—"

"Mahir, I am happy that you are in demand. Whenever you wish to leave, I will not stop you. I will not be a hurdle in anyone's progress."

I panicked. This conversation was going into uncharted territory.

"Ha—ha—ha." It was a forced laughter, only sounds coming from my mouth.

"What's so funny?"

"I, I think there has been a silly misunderstanding for which I apologize. I am never going to leave Elixir as long as you are my boss."

"Okay, I appreciate that. But that doesn't mean that your leave is approved, not for now at least."

●

The recruitment agency contact

"Do you have an appointment?" The pint sized secretary asked me. Sporting braces and a face covered with pimples, she looked more like a college student rather than an employee.

"Yes, Mr Ritwik himself asked me to see him today."

"Let me check, sir." The secretary ran her fingers, embellished with manicured, multicolored nails, on the desktop screen before replying gravely, "So sorry, sir. I cannot see your name here."

"Why don't you call him and check?" My irritation was beginning to show. I had not driven through two hours of excruciating traffic for a no show.

"I am sorry, sir. But Mr Ritwik is in a meeting; he cannot be disturbed right now. Why don't you take a seat, sir?"

"How much time will the meeting take?"

"Not too long, sir. Only about 15-20 minutes."

I waited for three long hours until I finally lost my patience and called up Ghoshal directly. The secretary didn't appreciate my direct approach, but Ritwik agreed to meet me.

As I stood next to Ritwik's cabin, I noticed that Ritwik was sitting alone. He greeted me warmly.

"Aah, come in Mahir. Hope you didn't have to wait too long? You know how these unplanned meetings happen." I had no idea, but I nodded my head in agreement. Ritwik continued, "A company CEO had come to see me for some help and I couldn't say no to an old friend. After all, I had given him the CEO's job."

I didn't see anyone coming out of Ritwik's cabin. However, I didn't want to mention this minor detail to the person who would be helping me find another job.

"So how can I help you, Mahir?"

"I am looking for a job change."

"Why do you want to change?"

"Oh, for better career prospects. I think I can do more justice to my potential by taking on new and bigger challenges. "

"Are you sure that the reasons are not more fundamental like inability to get along with the boss, low salary, ruthless work culture?"

Is Ritwik testing me? I hesitated a few seconds before replying. "No, nothing like that."

"You know, they say that people leave managers, not their companies."

I didn't volunteer a reply. Adhira would have been so proud of me that I didn't say something spontaneous. Ritwik looked a trifle disappointed.

"So Benoy referred me to you, eh? Loyal boy, that Benoy. I helped him get the job at Elixir after he was sitting at home for three months. You have come to the right place. My style of operation is quite different from the other recruitment agencies. I have a select clientele who consider me an extended HR arm of their companies. They outsource all their staffing requirements to me. I deal in only the very best. I don't just fill vacancies; I create new positions in these companies."

I was not sure as to how much of this was relevant to me but I was impressed. "Wow, that's fantastic, sir."

"No 'sir' business here. You can call me Ritwik, or Rits for short."

"Okay, Rits."

"Have you got your updated resume with you, Mahir?"

"Yes sir—I mean Ritwik—sorry, Rits." I handed over my resume folder to Ritwik.

As Ritwik browsed through the resume, he became pensive. "Hmmm…this resume is very basic, it will have to undergo a lot of improvements. You have to sell yourself to the client; your resume is the first and most important touchpoint. You have to treat your resume as an extension of your personality, if it doesn't appeal to the client in the first minute, you are out."

I was downcast. *All that money spent on improving my resume down the drain!*

"What should I do?"

"Don't worry, we will help you out."

The alarm bells in my head started ringing. My pockets were getting singed in this job search business.

"*Err,* how much will it cost me?"

Ritwik looked at me and smiled, as if reassuring a small child. "Relax, it will be free of charge. I believe in relationships, not transactions."

I breathed a sigh of relief. "Thank you, Rits."

"I can see that you are an engineer. Are you willing to work in a small company? It will be in this city only."

"Yes, of course."

"How would you like to get a managerial role with an almost 50-100% increase in pay?"

I felt elated. "Wow, that would be so amazing. I can't thank you enough."

"Don't thank me yet. But there is a problem. You don't have any managerial experience."

My shoulders drooped.

"But we can find a way to navigate this hurdle. I have some close contacts. All we have to do is pull the right strings."

I couldn't believe that a total stranger was going out of his way to help me. I felt like touching Ritwik's feet.

"Maybe if everything goes as per plan, you need not have to give an interview also. Usually, my word is final. Let's keep our fingers crossed."

"How can I ever thank you, Rits?"

Ritwik winked at me and said, "I am sure we will work out something later."

I went back home with a spring in my step, feeling supremely confident.

●

The Offer

I was missing Adhira. She was visiting her parents for a week. Considering that my leave did not materialize, this was a mutually accepted compromise. Adhira invited me to accompany her to her parents' house, but I deflected the invitation, citing office work. I was all alone in our house, fending for myself. The house was turning into a mess; I was beginning to dread Adhira's acerbic reactions on her return.

Nibbling on a cold paneer tikka masala pizza after a hard day's work, I saw my cellphone buzzing. It was Ritwik. There was no time to wash my hands. I took out my fingers from the pizza, wiped them on the curtains, and pressed the reply button.

"Rits?"

"Hey Mahir, guess what?"

My heart began pounding with anticipation, "I got the job?"

"Yep. Deputy Manager at Mexit Infotech, with a 200% pay hike. The best part of the job? Flexi time and both Saturday and Sunday off."

My jaw almost fell to the floor; this was too good to be true.

"Aren't you going to say something?"

I managed to find my voice. "It sounds incredible. How did you manage it?"

"There is a saying – enjoy the mangoes, don't count the trees. One small problem though. They want you to join immediately, no later than seven days. Think you can manage?"

"Of course, of course. I can join at this very hour if they want."

"Fantastic, I will inform them. And oh yes, I almost forgot to tell you. They need a copy your resignation letter, duly authorized by Elixir."

"I owe you, Rits."

"Yeah, big time." Ritwik laughed, before cutting the call.

I did a clumsy summersault in the house, missing the LCD TV by a whisker. I called up Adhira immediately.

"Hey baby, how are you doing?" Adhira asked in a lyrical tone of voice.

"I have something big to tell you, sweetie."

"Wait, don't tell me. Let me guess. You are coming to visit me?"

"No, that's not it. You know your parents don't like me. Living in with you hasn't exactly increased my popularity quotient with them."

"Hmmm… you cleaned the house all by yourself?"

"No, no… I mean yes, I did clean the house but that's not it."

"Then your leave got sanctioned finally?"

"Unfortunately not. Guess again."

"Oh baby, I give up. You tell me."

"I got a new job – Deputy Manager at Mexit Infotech. They want me to join in seven days."

"Wow, baby. That's really super news."

"Wish you were here with me right now. I wanted to celebrate with you. I am missing you, sweetie."

"I know baby, I am missing you badly too. Don't worry, just a couple of days more, then we will make up for lost time. I promise."

●

The exit

Almost half an hour had passed since the phone call from Khurana. I had been busy doodling in my notebook and looking at my watch repeatedly. I felt super confident, almost cocky as I strode upto Khurana's cabin with bold steps. He was almost frothing at the mouth as I entered his cabin. I cupped my mouth with my right hand to stop myself from smiling.

"What the hell is wrong with you? I told you to meet me a long time ago!" Khurana screamed at me.

"Yes sir, what could I do? I was finishing some important work."

The reply infuriated Khurana even more as he stood up and gestured with his hands animatedly. "How dare you? When I tell you to meet me, you should drop everything and come!" Khurana's voice was cracking up now.

I didn't reply this time, but I felt content.

"What the hell is happening to that Digibank report? I am getting reminders from them every hour."

"Sir, I am on it."

"On it? What does that mean? When are we giving them the report?"

"It will take some time, sir. I am short on resources."

"Oh come on! Always giving excuses. Haven't I told you so many times that this report was to be done on top priority?"

"Sir, I don't remember a single instance—"

"Please don't impose your poor memory on me. Can't I depend upon you to do a simple job?

"But sir, why are we giving so much importance to Digibank when they have not yet paid us for the last five assignments?"

"Why are you arguing with me unnecessarily? This is how a sale is done. Throw the bait. When the client bites, roll the hook in."

"But all the recent hooks on Digibank have been rolled in by our competitors. Digibank makes us do all the grunt work and gives the cream to someone else."

"And whose fault is that? It's useless trying to explain anything to you. Why don't you simply follow my instructions? Sometimes I feel that I made a catastrophic blunder by taking you on my team."

That was my trigger.

"Sir, if that is the way you feel, then I am going to leave, right here right now. "

"*Huh?*"

"But before I leave, I have to tell you something that I have been wanting to say for a very long time. You are the most self-seeking boss that I have ever worked with. You may say that I have worked with only one boss and how can I compare, but still. You have as much empathy or concern for your colleagues and subordinates as a hyena for his prey. Your leadership is so insipid and confusing. It's like taking two steps forward, three steps sideways, four steps backward and doing the hula hoop. You are an expert in identifying the smallest faults in a person and stretching them like rubber bands, as per your convenience. With you, the glass is never full – it is either half empty or completely empty."

Khurana was stunned, his jaw almost dropped to the floor. *Gosh, it felt exhilarating.*

"And for the record, I did not exactly sing your paeans in the Opinionated survey."

Khurana's mouth was still open with shock. There was an awkward silence in the room before Khurana found his voice. He looked terrified as he mumbled, "I – I – may have underestimated your stress levels. Perhaps you want to try meditation?"

I turned my back on Khurana and began to walk.

"I am okay if you need some more time to finish the Digibank report."

I slammed Khurana's cabin door on my way out. It felt like a rebirth.

●

Thanks with coffee

I was recounting my episode to Benoy at the chai ki tapri.

"That was awfully brave of you," remarked Benoy after he had heard me out.

My chest puffed up in pride. "I may look docile and weak but when someone does injustice to me, I am not going to grin and bear it."

"Hmmm… What next now? Did you meet up with Ritwik Ghoshal?"

"Arrey, I forgot to tell you. That Rits is really incredible."

"Rits?"

"Yes, he and I have become very good friends. He prefers to be called Rits."

"Okay."

"So Rits has found this amazing opportunity at Mexit Infotech, Deputy Manager with a 200% pay hike. That too without a formal interview. How cool is that?"

"Congratulations!"

"It's all credit to you, Benoy. After all, it was you who gave me the reference. Thanks a million."

"Aw, it was nothing really," remarked Benoy, handing me a glass of cutting chai.

"Err, enough of *chai*. Let's celebrate today. Shekhar, make two cups of special coffee for us. Your very best, eh."

"Sorry sir, no coffee today, only chai," replied the tapri stall boy disinterestedly.

●

Moment of truth

"I showed Khurana his true place today."

There was a long pause on my mobile phone after Adhira had heard out my resignation encounter with Khurana. She was still at her parents' place.

To fill the pause and hammer my point home, I re-iterated, "I may look docile and weak but when someone does injustice to me, I am not going to grin and bear it."

After another pause, I heard Adhira's voice; there was a palpable anxiety in the tone. "Just as I feared, sweetheart, what have you done?"

"*Huh,* what do you mean?" I asked, surprised.

"Baby, you have acted impulsively again."

"So what? I simply followed my heart."

"Baby, you are so simple and transparent."

"Thank you, sweetie."

"No, that was not a compliment, baby. Do you realize that Khurana has the power to stop all your HR clearances and stall your exit letter?"

I was speechless. The implications of my profound stupidity dawned upon me. "Oh my god, what have I done!"

"Exactly. And worse, you will not exactly get good references from Elixir now. Let us hope and pray that your new company doesn't do any reference check. Which reminds me, have you got the official appointment letter from Mexit Infotech?"

"Err, no, but Rits has assured me that the appointment letter is a mere formality, it will be issued any time now." My voice was no longer steady and confident.

"Oh my god! You put in your resignation at Elixir without even getting an official appointment letter from Mexit?"

I had already begun to panic.

●

Undo

"Hey, what are you trying to do?" asked Rajiv Goel, HR head at Elixir, who happened to be passing by.

"Can… can you not see that I am trying to open the door?" I replied in an irritated tone as I tried to catch my breath and ply Khurana's cabin door open.

"Why are you huffing and panting? Don't bother with the door, it's locked. Khurana is travelling out of the country. "

That's great! The one time I want to meet Khurana, he is out of the country. I had a brainwave. "Actually, you can help me out too, Rajiv."

Rajiv narrowed his eyes and asked warily, "What help?"

My tone pitch lowered to that of a whisper, "Did Khurana sir tell you anything unusual?"

"Hmmm… no, I don't think so."

The endorphins in my brain came to life, I felt a gush of relief. *The situation can still be salvaged.*

"—unless you are referring to your resignation." Anxiety gripped me again, tighter than ever.

"But… but it was just an overenthusiastic discussion with Khurana. I never gave any resignation."

"Oh yes, you have."

"No, I have not. Do you have anything in writing from me?"

"Oh, a written resignation is not required as per the company policy. We don't believe in bureaucracy. A verbal one is as good as a written one. Haven't you read the HR policies?"

"Err, no… but you guys never told me told me anything about this!"

"See, this is the fundamental problem. We take so much trouble in drafting HR policies and no one reads them. And then everyone blames HR."

"I am not blaming HR, Rajiv. There must be some way to take back the resignation? Please help me," I implored an impassive Rajiv.

Rajiv's eyes widened. "Take back your resignation? Sorry man, can't do that. Your resignation has already been accepted and processed."

I froze with horror. "But, but… how can you guys just accept somebody's resignation just like that? That too so quickly? Aren't you going to try and stop me?"

"We might have, but Mr Khurana explicitly instructed us to bypass the usual processes and relieve you immediately. He said that you were in a tearing hurry to go," Rajiv replied matter of factly.

"Arrey, there has been a huge misunderstanding. And, how can you just short-circuit the company processes just like that? What if I made a mistake?"

Rajiv tapped his chin with his forefinger.

"Well, you should have thought about it before, na? Are you saying that you made a mistake?"

"Of course not! I am only asking what if?"

"Can't help you there, you need to take it up with Mr Khurana directly. Unfortunately, we don't know when he will return."

●

Ritwik Ghoshal

"The number you are dialing, does not exist," the voice repeated like a parrot. *It does exist, you silly* *&^%$#@!

I grabbed a taxi and dashed towards Ritwik Ghoshal's office. I had barely entered the office when I noticed a familiar figure standing at the reception desk. Ritwik's secretary seemed to have grown a few inches taller, that too without heels. She seemed more womanly and mature now. Her hair had been dyed golden brown and there were no traces of pimples. I smiled at her, but she didn't reciprocate.

"How may I help you, sir?" The braces had disappeared too, the transformation was amazing.

"Don't you recognize me?"

"I am sorry sir, I don't. How may I help you, sir?"

"Is Rits in office?"

"Rits who?"

"Arrey, Ritwik Ghoshal!" I almost screamed.

"Mr Ritwik? Sorry sir, I have no idea."

"What do you mean you have no idea? You are sitting here, aren't you?"

"Sir, I don't think you have noticed the office board outside."

"No, why should I be interested in admiring your office board when I want to meet with Ritwik?"

"Sir, if you had read the board, you would have realized that this is the office of Chiman Patel Realtors."

"*Wha*—what? Where has Mr Ritwik gone?"

"How would I know?"

"But you have to know. After all, you worked for him, didn't you?"

"I think sir, you are confusing me for someone else."

I looked at the secretary closely this time. At least, now I had an explanation for the sudden height gain.

●

Mexit Infotech

"Welcome to Mexit Infotech. For Hindi, press 1. For Marathi, press 2. For Gujarathi, press 3. For Tamil, press 4. For Bengali, press 5. For Punjabi, press 6. For English, press 7."

I pressed the number 7.

"If you know the extension number of the person you are trying to reach, dial now. Or hold the line for operator assistance."

Someone switched on Indian classical music while I waited for the operator.

After about ten long minutes, the music was turned off and a lady's voice came on again. "We are sorry to keep you waiting. If you know the extension number of the person you are trying to reach, dial now. Or hold the line for operator assistance." The classical music was replayed, this time for fifteen whole minutes.

Finally, the lady's voice came back. "We are sorry to keep you waiting. But all lines are busy at the moment. Please try after some time. Thank you." *Click.*

I was not going to give up. I tried again and again and finally hit pay dirt on my *thirteenth* attempt.

"Mexit Infotech. How may I help you?"

"Could you connect me to someone in HR?"

"Sure sir. Whom should I connect you to?"

"Er, what's his name, name, name? Shucks, I can't seem to remember the name right now. But you can connect me to whosoever is in office right now."

"Sorry sir, I can't do that. You have to give me a name. Do you want to remember and then call us back?"

I was horrified at the thought of having to call back again. "No… I mean no. Wait, I think I remember. His name starts with H, he is very jovial and he speaks fluent English."

"There is no one at Mexit matching that description, sir."

"Wait, I think I made a mistake, his name starts with P."

"No sir."

"How about B?"

"No sir."

"D?"

"Sir, we don't have time to go through all twenty-six letters like this. I really need to—"

I was about to cry. "Ma'am, I need your help, please ma'am."

"Okay, okay. I will connect the call to a junior intern at HR. Hold on, sir."

"Thank you so much."

"Abhishek Diwan here. Who is this?"

"Hello sir. My name is Mahir Adwait. I have been recently appointed at Mexit, but I have not yet received my appointment letter."

"Really? Who took your interview?"

"Sir, no one took my interview, but I was told that I had been hired."

"Hahaha. Nice joke, sir. We never hire without taking interviews first. We also never recruit without issuing appointment letters."

"Sir, I am not joking. You can ask Mr Ritwik Ghoshal. Surely you know him?"

There was a long pause at the other end of the phone, followed by an audible sigh. "So you have come through Ritwik's reference, eh?"

"Yes sir, yes sir," I replied enthusiastically.

"No wonder."

"No wonder what?"

"You see, Ritwik's agency's contract has been terminated by Mexit."

My mind went numb. "T-terminated? W-why?"

"It's confidential. Let's just say that he had become too big for his boots. The HR guy from Mexit, liaising with Ritwik, has also been fired. All appointments made through Ritwik have been rescinded. Did you pay any money to Ritwik?"

"No, he never asked me for money."

"Consider yourself very lucky."

"Lucky? Why lucky?"

"Well, there are candidates from whom Ricky has charged two to five lakh rupees. The worst hit are those candidates who had been issued appointment letters and had been working at Mexit. Not only have they been fired, but Mexit has asked them to repay the salaries paid to them over the last few month, with interest."

It was all over. I disconnected the call.

A month later - Second thoughts

My eyes were still closed when Adhira rushed next to my bedside excitedly with a steaming cup of tea and the day's newspaper. "Hey baby, get up, get up, get up!"

I opened one eye, extended a hand to take the cup of tea and said groggily, "Thank you, sweetie. You shouldn't have bothered, really."

"This tea is for me, not you. But check out today's newspaper."

Not interested. I was about close both eyes and go back to sleep, but Adhira had begun to read. *"Elixir solutions declares record profits, employees set to reap windfall with generous pay hikes and stock options."*

I sprung up from my bed, wide awake now. I had already anticipated what Adhira was about to say next – *Quitting Elixir was a big mistake.*

"Quitting Elixir was a big mistake, baby."

●

Return of the prodigal

I was still unemployed after three months. After continuous begging, pleading, emailing, messaging, apologizing and a string of unreturned phone calls, I had still not managed to cut the ice with Jagmohan Khurana.

I decided to risk it and confront him in office. Not that I had much to lose besides my tattered pride and self dignity.

My legs felt heavy, I was sweating, my heart palpitating. I was entering the crocodile's lair of my own accord. I noticed that the reptile had a spanking new metallic name plate riveted onto his cabin door. 'Shri Jagmohan Khurana, President'. Reluctantly, I knocked on Khurana's cabin door, secretly hoping he was too busy to meet me. *Too late, I was spotted!*

"Ah, Mahir, come in, come in. What a pleasant surprise. What brings you here?"

My stupidity, for which I am going to regret very soon.

"I am doing great, sir. It's just that I felt like dropping by and saying hello to you, so here I am."

"Good, good."

"So how are you doing sir?"

"Not bad, not bad at all."

Of course, you would say that, you swine, with the undeserved promotion and god knows how many crores of stock options.

"Where have you taken up a job now?"

"Actually sir, I got a number of very good offers, great position, great salaries, but I turned them all down."

Khurana looked at me incredulously. "Aaah, why is that?"

This was the toughest part. I pinched myself, swallowed my spit, lowered my head, put on my most believable face and replied, "Sir, I realized that I missed your leadership and this company atmosphere. So I came here wondering if I could rejoin—"

"Hmmm… I knew that you had taken a hasty decision and even tried to stop you."

When the hell did you try to stop me?

"Do you know that I had recommended your name for a promotion before you—"

"Sir, I would be so honoured."

"Yeah, yeah. But this is no longer relevant now."

Damn! At least I tried.

"Sir, no… no problem. I… *uh*… am willing to rejoin at my old salary and designation."

"Hmmm, there is a problem. Your vacancy no longer exists; it had been filled up immediately. But I will keep you in mind in case any suitable opportunity comes up."

It has been hardly three months and you have already found my replacement?

"Could I know who has joined in my place?"

"I don't know if you know him. His name is Benoy Gupta."

Turbulence

"*Jai Shri Krishna! Jai Shri Krishna! Jai Shri Krishna! Jai Shri Krishna! Jai Shri Krishna!*"

I prayed fervently, my general religious antipathy, replaced by a renewed belief in the Almighty. My stomach was churning viciously; it seemed as if my guts would pop out of my stomach, as I held on to my arm rests in an iron clad grip.

"I am too young to die. I have so much to achieve in life. Please have pity on me and save me today, my lord."

There was no respite; the aircraft kept quivering violently like a pneumatic compressor making sudden turns, ignoring the screams of the roaring jet engines, which threatened to give away any second. The plane's metal were being subjected to extreme torsional stresses. I was unable to dismiss undesirable thoughts of the liner being torn apart in mid air.

The pilot and the crew were conspicuously silent. Something must have been seriously amiss. I glanced at my fellow passengers and noticed that the majority of the faces had been flushed white, stricken with foreboding. Some were peering outside their windows continuously, apparently trying to figure out what was going on. Some sat with their eyes closed, presumably meditating to relieve the stress or making silent appeals to their respective gods. Anxious chants of *Allah hu Akbar* could be heard from a few quarters. Couples held hands and hugged each other. A couple of kids were bawling incessantly, a definitive ill omen. Had it not been for the seat belts, I would have done some screaming myself at the parents of these kids for being unable to keep them under control.

Amidst all the chaos and clamor, I heard a distinct snoring sound, akin to a two-stroke petrol engine. I turned around and looked; it was my co-passenger, the country bumpkin. The *damn* fellow was sleeping without a care in the world. *What the *&^%\$^&!*

Pleading with the top management in heaven was not helping; I needed to demonstrate my faith. Joining my hands together and looking upwards at the overhead storage bins, I made a solemn promise. "I promise to give up alcohol." The higher powers were apparently not too impressed; there was no improvement in the flying conditions.

"Okay, I will also visit the temple, once in a while," I said aloud, congratulating myself mentally for not making any time commitment.

At that very moment, there were three heart-stopping strikes of lightening, in rapid succession. I decided to increase the stakes. I had been planning for a long time now to give back to society, this was my chance. "If the plane lands safely, I promise to donate 5% of my earnings to charity. No, make that 10%." With an immediate afterthought, I added, "Sorry, make that 7%." *It was a very tough decision made under duress; I could not afford to be rash.*

After a few more hair-raising moments, there was a glimmer of hope as the turbulence appeared to subside palpably. I continued my conversation with the Lord.

"Thank you, Shri Krishna, for finally listening to your humble servant. With your permission, I wanted to elaborate a little on my promises so that there is no misunderstanding between us later. With regards to the earlier promise of giving up alcohol, since you didn't like it, I will presume that the same stands cancelled. And with regards to giving my money to charity, this will be from my post tax earnings in post dated cheques, ten years from now. Just to clarify.

Thank you, Shri Krishna, for being so understanding."

One of my traits that I have always prided myself on is my presence of mind, as I silently patted myself on my back.

And then, without warning, the plane dived. This was the last straw *(technically the second last)*, I screamed *(along with many others, if I may add)*.

One hour ago.

"Excuse me, you are sitting on my seat," I said, not attempting to disguise my irritation. Almost missing my flight, I had been the last passenger to check in after a lot of imploring and cajoling with the hardnosed airline authorities. And then, it had been a series of serpentine queues for me, at the security check-in line and thereafter the boarding line. The airport was more crowded than the local railway station. And now, when it was time to finally relax my tired legs, this idiot had plonked himself on it.

"Oh! This is the first time I am flying, you see. I thought we could sit on any seat we wanted?"

Of all the &^%$#! Where did this guy come from?*

I looked at him closely. He was a wiry youth, wearing a cheap leather jacket, unbranded jeans and vanilla white ked shoes *(probably purchased as part of a package deal from a home shopping channel)*. He had oily, wavy hair and sported a *rudraksha* bracelet on his right hand.

"No, we can't. Each seat has a number. You have to match the number with the number on your boarding pass." Flashing my boarding pass at his nose, I said icily, "My seat number is 9C, as in A-B-C."

"Aah! I am sorry. I will give up this seat for you," the guy declared grandiosely before shuffling across to the adjacent seat.

Was this guy thick in the head or just hard of hearing?

"No, no, you need to sit on your seat, not just any seat you like. Please show me your boarding card." The guy dutifully gave his card to me.

"Look mister, it says here that your seat is... aahh... 9B." I fumbled for a second and then added in a low tone, "Okay, you can continue to sit on that seat."

"Thank you sir," the fellow replied cheerfully. Then he unhooked the seat tray table, extracted five figurines of various popular deities from his duffel bag, and placed it on the tray. Bowing to the figurines, he tapped the feet of each figurine with his right hand, and then tapped his forehead with the same hand.

Weirdo!

I realized that I was staring at the guy, when he suddenly produced a small sachet of *suji halwa* from nowhere. "*Prasad?*" he asked.

Sheesh, how old is that? And is it even hygienic?

"Er no, thank you." *I am not about to risk food poisoning.*

"You should never say no to *prasad*. Keep it."

I took the sachet reluctantly and popped it into the seat pocket in front of me, when the guy was not looking. I suspected that the guy would try to start a conversation and get all friendly. To prevent this possibility, I took out the morning newspaper from the pocket and pretended to read. Alas—

"Hi, my name is Vasudev Javdekar. I am a poultry farmer from Sangli. Do you know Sangli? It is only 370 kilometres from Mumbai. You must visit Sangli sometime and stay in my house. I have about five thousand chickens and two tractors."

Good for you, you can count your chickens while they hatch. I couldn't care less.

Ignoring him, I tried to focus on my reading:

'*Indian Government copyrights the term – Surgical strike, bans unauthorized usage.*'

'*President Donald Trump impeached.*'

'*Flipkart declares bankruptcy despite getting US$ 1.2 billion in a fresh round of funding.*'

'*India gets seat on security council.*'

'*Arvind Kejriwal gives up PM bid and settles for chief ministership of Bihar, cries conspiracy.*'

Same old staid news as usual, utter rubbish! I missed *The Times of India* and its page 3 news, juicy gossip about movie stars, latest movie reviews and my favourite – The Astrology section.

"—Business is becoming tougher by the day, with some kind of flu being discovered every second day and the poor chickens being blamed for them. I also have a dairy farming business, but that is not doing too well, quality of hay is deteriorating by the day—"

How do I get this chatter express to shut up?

I was about to press the flight attendant call button for help. But before I could do so, a tall svelte figure in uniform, swaying hair, slits for eyes pointing upwards, northeastern features, appeared next to me.

"Wow, that was amazing, technology has really advanced nowadays."

The sweet lady smiled and replied, "We try to delight the customer, sir."

For a fleeting moment, I thought she was being sarcastic, but I brushed away the thought; she was too pretty to be mean. My neighbour had pressed the pause button, so the interim objective was achieved.

"Sir, as you are sitting next to the emergency exit, I need to brief you on the emergency procedures. During the unlikely event of an emergency landing, pull that red knob on the emergency door downwards and throw the door. Do not stow anything under your seats as it blocks the exit path. You can read the rest of the safety instructions kept in the seat pocket in front of you. Sir, you will need to keep that duffel bag in the overhead storage."

I protested, pointing towards the chicken farmer. "This bag is not mine, it is his."

"I am sorry, ma'am. I will keep the bag," my companion spoke up. For a village hillbilly, the guy seemed to be surprisingly polished.

The veil dropped, when he opened his mouth again.

"*Er,* could you ask the driver to drive carefully? This is my first trip, you see."

"Don't worry sir, the pilot is highly experienced," replied the airhostess with a straight face.

"Could you ask him to check the engine oil, fuel meter and tyre pressure? I always check these three things before driving my tractor."

"Sure sir, I will convey your message," said the airhostess, throwing funny looks at both me and my companion.

I rolled my eyes and remonstrated. "Hey, I am not with him."

The chicken farmer was not yet done with his laundry list of questions. "What if this door suddenly opens in mid air?"

Gawd, such a birdbrain!

"It's a good question," the airhostess commented.

Was it? Maybe it was a good question after all. I had myself thought of it so many times.

"It is almost impossible for the door to open outward during mid air flight because of internal air pressure in the cabin. In any case, we advise passengers to keep their seat belts on at all times. But don't worry, sir, Connected Airlines maintains the highest safety standards," replied the air hostess in all seriousness.

"Being chicken comes naturally to the chicken farmer," I remarked wryly and began to laugh, but stopped abruptly, when I saw that that the other two hadn't understood the joke.

I craned my neck to get a closer look closely at the name tag pinned on the upper part of the airhostess's dress.

"Did you want something, sir?" asked the air hostess icily.

I was puzzled by the cold greeting and then it struck me as I looked at her in horror. "No, no, no, I wasn't looking at your... I mean, your name is Mharoni?."

"Yes sir, that's what it says on the name tag. Now, did you want something? I need to attend to other passengers also," said the lady, with an irritated undertone.

"You have a nice name, it is quite unique," I replied with my best smile. Instead of thanking me or reciprocating my compliment, Mharoni simply turned her back on me on walked off.

Some people could be so rude. What's her problem?

"Say, you haven't told me anything about yourself." It was my *chipku* neighbour again.

Buzz off mate; I am in no mood right now.

"What is your name?"

"Uh-huh, Tom Cruise." I had no motivation to reveal my real name, Ghyanchand Manchandani.

"*Aah* Tom Cruise, that name sounds familiar. Have we met before?"

Duh.

"I don't think so."

"You have a great personality, Tom. You must be a big company *sahib*, na?"

The first astute observation.

"Yes, I am the Senior Manager in a huge pest control company."

"*Aha*, I knew it! "

"I always travel business class, but today, seats were not available."

"Do you mean the big seats in the front of the plane? But I saw that they are all empty."

"No, no, they are not empty. The passengers must have gone to the washroom."

"You seem to be an experienced and knowledgeable traveller, Tom. This is my first flight—"

"I know, I know."

"I wanted to ask you something, Tom. There are more people sitting behind on this plane, the front seats are almost empty. Should we not be asking the driver to shift some people from back to the front? What if the plane loses its balance?"

What an incredulous thought! Whoever had even heard of such a thing? Unbalanced plane, ha! I am sure that the plane must be designed for this. On second thoughts, is it? Even if isn't, the pilot and the crew would have surely taken care of it. Or have they? God, this guy is messing with my brain.

I had to clear the nagging thought once and for all. My forefinger moved towards the flight attendant button and hovered for a few seconds. No one came. I had to press it five times before Mharoni appeared in front of us.

"Hey Mharoni, so nice to see you again."

"That attendant button is not a toy that you keep pressing it repeatedly, sir," Mharoni rebuked me severely. "Did you want something, sir, or are you going to keep flirting with me and wasting my time?"

I went red in the face. *Who does this female think she is? Miss Universe? &^%$#*&!*

"I didn't mean to upset you; I am sorry. This gentleman here wanted to ask you a very important question."

"No sir, I don't want to ask her anything," my irritating neighbour replied immediately, turning his face away.

"But, you just asked me——"

"It's okay, sir."

*What a *&^%$! Now he gets cold feet. I will just have to ask her myself.*

"*Ah* Mharoni… uh…er… is there any danger of the plane getting unbalanced because of the uneven seating of the passengers?"

Mharoni seemed alarmed and amused. "Whoever gave you such an idea, sir?"

"It was him, not me. I knew it was a stupid question, but this guy was pestering me——"

"No sir, I meant that it is an interesting thought. Nobody has asked me this question before."

Make up your goddamn mind.

"I think they load the entire luggage and the fuel in the front to balance the plane."

I began to laugh, but cut it short when I saw Mharoni's curt look in my direction. She was apparently not joking.

Time to change the topic. "Ahem, can I get a bottle of—" It was pointless, Mharoni had turned her back towards me again. I felt like shouting behind her back. *Your back is not as attractive as your front.*

"That lady gets upset quickly, na?" my neighbour commented.

"Why did you back off like that, man?"

"Sorry sir. But this is my first flight, sir. And I am so jittery."

"I know, I know. Just relax. Statistically speaking, air travel is the safest form of travel."

"That's what they tell me, sir. But I also hear that the survival rate is almost zero, if something actually happens. You sir, must have travelled so much. Don't you ever get scared of flying?"

"Naah, it is all in the mind really. When something has to happen, it will happen. The important thing to remember is keep calm even if something goes wrong. There was this one time during one of my long haul flights, when I noticed that the engine had caught fire. I immediately informed the stewards but they started panicking. So I took the initiative and intimated the pilot about the danger. I advised him to take deep breaths and to not get worried. "

"Wow, what did the pilot say?"

"He said 'Get out of my cockpit'. I am sure he meant to say thank you, but he was very nervous."

"And then?"

"I also reassured the passengers on the plane that things would be okay. Many of them thanked me later, saying that had it not been for me, they would have never known about the problem."

"Wow, what happened after that?"

"The flight landed safely and we all went home."

"You are so courageous; you are the Master, Tom Cruise."

"Oh, it was nothing, really. I was just doing my service to humanity, an ordinary person doing an extraordinary job. Courage was incidental," I added in all humility.

Half an hour ago, after a smooth flight take off

"Hello sir, would you like to have vegetarian or non vegetarian?" It was Mharoni standing next to us along with a meal tray.

"Hi Mharoni, destiny has brought us together again. How's that for a co-incidence, *eh?*"

"I will have vegetarian," my neighbour interrupted. I looked at him in surprise. *What the—*

"What is the cost for one tray?" he asked.

Once a bumpkin, always a bumpkin.

"Oh, the tray is absolutely free, sir."

"In that case, can I get two trays? I have a big appetite, you see."

I couldn't help smirking. "This is not a buffet. You get only one meal at one time. Am I right, Mharoni?"

Mharoni waited me to finish before replying to my neighbour. "Sure sir, we can get you one extra tray. No problem at all."

That wiped the smile off my face. *All this time, I had the wrong idea. Well, what do you know. Let me try my luck also.*

"Er, Mharoni, I am feeling rather hungry too. Can I get two trays also, please? Only non-vegetarian for me, please."

"Sorry sir, we have run out of non vegetarian trays," replied Mharoni, maintaining her poise.

Back to the present

It was a free fall. There was a loss in cabin pressure and the oxygen masks dropped. The seat belt signs were flashing now.

I was a trifle upset with the Lord for enabling me to catch this flight instead of missing it this one time, but this was not the time to voice my angst aloud. My inclination towards religion had grown exponentially in the last few minutes, as I repeatedly took the name of the Lord, making up for lost time in the last two decades. In the midst of the chanting, I glanced at my neighbour; he was still in *la la* dreamland. *How could someone sleep so comfortably at a time like this?* Notwithstanding the stressful situation, I took it upon myself to wake up the guy and make him aware of the peril. I nudged him repeatedly, but that didn't have any effect. I then shook him hard. Letting out occasional grunts, he simply rolled over from side to side, blissfully ignorant.

As I lunged past my neighbour and looked out of the window, all I could see were tufts of dense clouds, stretched as far as my vision would go. The plane was flying over the Arabian Sea at that moment, not exactly the kind of place I would have wanted the plane to make an emergency landing.

I extracted the safety instructions card and tried to read it, but my hands were shivering and my brain had gone numb. I cursed myself for having never heeded flight attendant's safety demonstrations in the past. To make matters worse, the undigested meal in my stomach was bouncing around like crazy; I felt that I could puke any second. It was then, when I started to cry uncontrollably.

It would be all over, soon. I was seized with regret and remorse as the following thoughts breezed through my head.

- I wish I had repaid the loan for which my bank was pursuing me for the last ten years.
- I wish I had handed in my resignation letter and told my boss to F*** O**.
- I wish I had said sorry to my friend, with whom I had fought and not spoken to in the last fifteen years (couldn't remember though why we had fought in the first place).
- I wish I had taken a life insurance policy.

As I shed copious tears, the plane began to get back some semblance of control and stabilize. *There was hope after all, praise the Lord.* I was experiencing the oft-repeated adage – God works in mysterious ways. I didn't know how, but I was sure that my tears were somehow responsible for the plane limping back to normalcy. Finally, after what seemed like eternity, the clouds had disappeared and the vibrations subsided. I finally stopped crying when the seat belt signs came off *(didn't want to stop crying in between and tempt fate again).*

Five minutes later, there was an announcement. "Good afternoon ladies and gentlemen, this is your captain speaking."

High time you came on, mister!

"We are cruising at 30, 000 feet and will be making our descent shortly, as we approach Oman."

Are you kidding?

"The weather in the city is sunny and pleasant, with the temperature at 23 deg centigrade. We hope that you have a pleasant stay in the city and give an opportunity to Connected Airlines to serve you again soon."

The impudence of the pilot, not even a word of apology from the rascal! I am disconnecting Connected Airlines forever.

I heard strange sounds. "*Oohaahoooh---yaaawn---*" It was my neighbour; he was finally waking up from his slumber.

"Aaah, looks like we are about to reach, eh?"

I shot an incredulous look at the man. His movements were slow and lazy, his face calm, relaxed and content, as he stretched his arms and legs.

"Your face seems wet and your eyes red, Tom. Is everything all right?"

Embarrassed and acutely conscious, I wiped off my soggy face with a tissue paper.

"Yes, yes…something entered my eyes. But tell me, how did you manage to sleep through such terrible air turbulence?"

"Hmmm…I don't know about air turbulence. But I guess it felt like I was like sitting on my own tractor; didn't realize when I fell asleep. Quite relaxing, I have to say. "

Relaxing?? Did I hear that right?

"You were right, Tom. Air travel is quite safe and comfortable. I was worrying unnecessarily. Thank you for reassuring me."

Definitely a weirdo!

Arrival

No sooner had the plane touched down on the runaway, joyous shouts could be heard all across the aisles. Springing up from my seat, I opened the overhead bin to extract the luggage, and exit the plane at the first possible opportunity.

The plane speakers crackled to life, as another announcement was made. "Passengers are requested to remain seated and keep their seat belts fastened till the plane comes to a stop. You are advised not to rush, as everyone will be getting off at the same time."

To hell with your announcements. I am getting off right now. Stop me if you can.

A stern looking male steward walked up to me and beckoned me to stay seated. It was not a request, but an order. Looking at the fellow's size and comparing it with mine, I took the wise decision of sitting down.

As the plane ground to a halt, all the passengers stood up and formed a queue at the aisle to exit the plane. I tried to shake off my *chipku* companion, but he stuck to my side. Walking slowly, my heart gladdened when I noticed Mharoni greeting the passengers at the exit. This would be my last chance. Changing my strategy, I waited until all the passengers got off the plane. As I approached Mharoni, I smiled at her, in one last desperate attempt to melt the ice queen. "Hope we meet again some time." And then I took a shot in the dark. "Can I get your phone number, please?" I asked in a low trembling tone.

Mharoni gave me a sweet plastic smile. "Goodbye Mr Ghyanchand. Hope you will fly with us again."

"Of course, of course. I will become a frequent flyer with Connected Airlines."

"Er, ma'am, his name is Tom Cruise, not Mr Ghyanchand." My unwanted companion was speaking up for me. *Who asked for your opinion?*

"Oh, is it? My mistake, sorry." Mharoni eyes arched upwards as she covered her mouth with her hands and made funny noises. I could have sworn that she was sniggering.

My pride hurt, I tried to make a recovery. I tried to get close to Mharoni and whisper. "Ahem... he is a village yokel. Don't take him seriously."

Mharoni ignored me and focused on my companion. "I couldn't help but notice that you were the only passenger who was not bothered at all with the rough flight. You are a brave man, sir." she chirped.

"Oh, that was nothing."

I burned with envy. *Since when did ignorance get categorized as bravery?*

"Sir, these are for you," Mharoni announced, thrusting a hamper of chocolates into the duffer's outstretched hands.

I spotted a few extra hampers kept on an elevated tray behind Mharoni. "Can I get some of these chocolates too? They will be special, coming from you."

Mharoni gave me a deadpan expression. "Sorry sir, these chocolates are for special occasions only." Adding insult to my injury, she added, "But you can buy the chocolates at any airport confectionary shop. You need to move ahead sir, we have to close the doors and prepare the plane for the next flight."

The Pitch

I was reading my morning newspaper at leisure when Ayesha barged into the room and snatched the paper rudely from my hand.

"Hey, I was reading—" I began to protest.

"I am calling out to you for so long, the least you can do is give a proper reply instead of giving *hmmms* and *aaahs*." With almond shaped, kohl lined eyes, Ayesha was still attractive after eleven years of marriage. *Except on such occasions.*

"Hmmm."

Ayesha sighed. "Do you ever listen to a word I say in the house, Burhan?"

"Of course, my dear."

"Okay then, what was I saying?"

"You were saying… *uh…* why don't you tell me again in that sweet voice of yours? I love to hear it again and again."

"Cut the crap," Ayesha admonished me. "I have news from Azaan's school."

"What? Has the duffer failed in yet another exam? No wonder you are in such a bad mood. I have been telling you that sending

Azaan to a private school is a complete waste of money. We still have time to shift him to a government school and save some money for our Europe trip."

Ayesha looked at me, exasperated. "How can you talk about our only son like this? For your information, there was some kind of national talent exam held in his school and Azaan was one of the few children who qualified for a scholarship."

I was shocked."That's impossible. Did you check how many students gave the exam in the first place?"

"Are you not listening? I already told you that it was a national talent exam, which means students from all over India would have—"

"Yes, yes, but I find it very difficult to believe. Maybe these fellows mixed up the names? "

"Can you show some faith in Azaan, for once?"

"I do have complete faith in Azaan. In fact, I am sure that the following three things will never happen in my lifetime – a snake and a mongoose becoming friends, the moon becoming blue and Azaan getting good marks."

"Burhan, he is your own son, for Allah's sake."

"I wonder about that also, at times. For all you know, someone might have switched babies at the hospital?"

"*Burhan!*"

"I mean, Azaan keeps disappointing us. I should have been a role model for him, but he prefers to idolize those wrestling morons in silly costumes instead."

"Why should he idolize you? You weren't that bright in studies either."

"Aah, maybe I wasn't bright, but I was always intelligent, there is a subtle difference. There is no need to grin, okay?"

"Listen Burhan, I have received a letter from the school which says there will be a felicitation ceremony for all those kids who have qualified for the scholarship next weekend, in the evening, at Shanmukhananda hall. Will you take us there?"

"Shanmukhananda hall? That's *soooo* far away, it's almost like out of town."

"Cut the drama. It's only twenty kilometres from our house."

"But Ayesha, it's on a weekend. It's the one day I get to sit at home and relax. Is it really necessary for me to go? I will cheer for Azaan, from home."

Ayesha looked at me incredulously. "Burhan, this is Azaan's first big achievement; I have already told all our friends and relatives. You are taking us to Shanmukhananda hall next weekend and that is final, okay?"

"Can I first see Azaan's letter?"

"Here, have a look at this." I grabbed the letter from Ayesha's hands and began to read.

"This is incredible!"

"Of course! That is what I have been trying to tell you."

"No, I meant that these fellows are offering a five star buffet dinner, completely free!"

One week later

The program had been delayed by over an hour as huge serpentine queues were still making their way into the Shanmukhananda auditorium. It was dark and crowded inside, with silhouettes of various hues bobbing all over the place. We were fortunate to have located a few vacant seats amidst the jamboree, with the help of the torchlight at the tip of my mobile phone.

I tapped Ayesha on her shoulder. "Can you pass me the water bottle please?"

"What do you think are you doing, mister?" An irritated and unrecognizable female voice spoke up.

"Oops, so sorry," I apologized sheepishly.

"I am *here,* on your right," Ayesha hissed, as she passed me the bottle of water.

My six-year-old Zaira tugged at my shirt impatiently. "Papa, I want ice cream."

"Not now dear. Later."

"I want ice cream," Zaira repeated defiantly.

"But dear, no one is selling ice cream here."

"I want ice cream."

I remembered that I had a couple of candies in my pocket. I took out the candies and offered them to Zaira. She readily took the candies from my hand and repeated, "I want ice cream."

Ayesha was conspicuously silent.

"Ayesha, can you please help me out here?"

"It's so hot in here, isn't it? Wonder if the central air conditioner is working—"

"Papa, I am so bored. Can I get your mobile? I want to play some games." It was Azaan's turn to make a demand.

"Bored? Doing what? Sorry. There are only a few sticks of power left on my phone, I don't want you to waste them by playing games."

"Papa, I want ice cream." Zaira had not budged from her position.

The stage lights were switched on as a microphone stuttered to life.

A grave voice announced grimly. "All rise for the national anthem, please."

"What is the need to play the national anthem right now?" I grumbled.

Ayesha and the kids stood up promptly.

"Stand up, Burhan," Ayesha hissed.

"Relax, no one can see us. *Owwww*, why are you pinching me?"

No sooner than the last word of the anthem was uttered, I plonked myself on my seat.

The spotlight was switched on and focused upon a young lady no older than twenty-five years old. Dressed in a dapper, svelte purple gown with daring cuts, the lady took centre stage.

"Good evening children, ladies and gentlemen. I am Danielle, your host for the evening. Before we start, please give yourselves a big round of applause, ladies and gentlemen." I clapped heartily to demonstrate my solidarity with the hostess.

Ayesha was not too impressed. "Why are you standing, Burhan?" she hissed.

I sat down on my seat obediently.

"Isn't that outfit a tad too revealing?" Ayesha asked aloud.

I avoided eye contact with Ayesha and said innocently. "What outfit, dear? I hadn't noticed."

"Today is a historic day," Danielle continued. "We have gathered here today to recognize the brilliant young children from across different corners of India. After a nationwide hunt scouting for talent spread across 26 states and numerous schools, using a complex and state of the art algorithm, we have identified children with precocious talent.

"For all those parents who are seated here today, you will be proud to know that your children are the *chosen* ones. "

I leaned across and whispered to Ayesha. "Our Azaan has precocious talent? Haha. God knows what algorithm these fellows have used."

"*Shh*... listen."

"The children will be felicitated today by our special chief guest for the evening, Mr Kriyansh Sakhrani or Mr KS as he likes to be called."

The spotlight shifted focus briefly upon an expressionless guy in his early thirties, tussled hair, attired in a skin-tight orange T-shirt and low rise blue denims. The guy seemed to have stepped straight out of the gym with his abs bulging out from beneath his tight T-shirt.

Ayesha's eyes were transfixed on the fellow. I leaned towards Ayesha again and opened my mouth. Without shifting her gaze, she said tersely, "Shhh."

The spotlight focus shifted back to Danielle. "A go getter since a very early age, Mr KS has the rare distinction of clearing all the toughest exams in India, IIT, UPSC, CAT in a span of only ten years. In the IIT admission exam, he secured the 5894th position in the third attempt itself. For the UPSC exam, he cleared all the mock tests, but was unable to appear for the main exam, as he was struck with an unfortunate bout of diarrhea on the fated day. In CAT, he secured 80 percentile and almost got a seat at one of the prestigious IIMs."

"Why did he give so many exams, papa?" Azaan asked me innocently.

"*Shhh...* listen."

"Looking at Mr KS's success, his friends approached him for help in clearing competitive exams. While helping out his friends, Mr KS had a Eureka moment and took a life-changing decision. He decided that he would give back to society by devoting his life to teaching.

I would now like to invite Mr KS to the stage and say a few words. Request everyone in the audience to remain seated, tea and snacks will be served at the end of the program."

I leaned towards Ayesha and whispered, "Only tea and snacks? I thought they had promised a free five star dinner?"

Ayesha rolled her eyes and exclaimed, "Yes yes. Why are you getting so impatient?"

"But why are they not talking about it yet? I am beginning to feel hungry—"

"Sshh... listen."

"Everyone, please give it up for Mr KS."

Amidst the applause from the crowd, the expressionless guy with the skin tight T-shirt walked up in a casual manner towards Danielle and took over the mike.

"Thank you, Danielle, for that nice introduction. If you don't mind, could you stand back a little? Thank you. I don't want people to get distracted when I am speaking.

Unfortunately, what I have to share with this august audience here cannot be encapsulated in a few words. But before I begin, I have to point out a few corrections in your speech. First of all, I do not like to be called Mr KS. Shortening one's name is a sign of disrespect to someone's identity. Moreover, abbreviations are subject to multiple interpretations. Second of all, I did not have diarrhea at the time of the UPSC exam; I had chicken pox. Thirdly, I secured 82 percentile in the CAT exam, not 80 percentile."

"Papa, what does CAT exam mean?" Azaan asked me.

"Don't ask such silly questions. It's basic general knowledge, you should know this. CAT stands for Chartered Accountancy Test."

"No, no, it stands for Common Aptitude Test," Ayesha butted in without invitation.

"Yes, maybe. Depends upon how you want to interpret it, Azaan." Azaan had already stopped listening.

"Papa, I don't want ice cream now. I want a cat," Zaira announced.

"Hold your horses, Zaira." I said exasperatedly.

"I don't want a horse. I want a cat."

Kriyansh continued in the same vein. "Looking at my success, many of my friends approached me for guidance. When some of my friends began clearing these competitive exams as well, then it struck me, why don't I share my knowledge with the world and shape the life of millions, instead of a handful? It was almost six years ago, that the seed of my company Genius was sown. In these six years, Genius has grown at breakneck speed from 5 students to over 250, 000 students now."

I leaned towards Ayesha again and whispered. "What a *phenku!*"

"Shhh… listen."

I'd had enough. "What's with all this *shhhing* business?"

"Shhhhh."

"The unique proposition of Genius is that we use digital technology as a teaching platform. Instead of conventional tuition teachers and physical classrooms, Genius offers the flexibility of studying in any place with a Wi-Fi network, at a fraction of the traditional cost. Our entire teaching concept is based on the adage: Fun while you learn. We combine the joy of mobile gaming with the knowledge of books. All you need is a tablet and a pre-loaded SD card. The entire learning will be in Virtual 3D, children will be given special 3D glasses. At the end of every class, there is a fun game to test the learning. The names of the top 100 scorers are flashed across the country."

"Papa, I want a cat."

"Uh-huh—"

"Our statistics have shown that for those using the Genius package,

a. Children are thrice as likely to improve their concentration as compared to children attending a physical classroom or tuition class.

b. Fights between parents and children involving repeated requests/ threats by parents to their wards to study, reduce by 90%. Children study of their own accord.

c. There is at least 50% probability of improvement in performance of a child, by an average of 0.1%."

Who cares? Where is he going with all this?

Zaira was tugging at my shirt again. "Papa, cat!"

Kriyansh paused as a solitary slide was projected on the stage background screen. The slide looked something like this *(attempt to reproduce from memory, source: Genius Education).*

Kriyansh pointed his index finger at the slide and averred, "To put it in a nutshell, this slide shows you the benefits of using the Genius package, especially for children seated in this auditorium."

Realization dawned upon me. *We had been ambushed. All this drama was nothing more than a massive sales pitch.*

Ayesha looked at me and giggled. "That image on the top left reminds me of someone rushing to catch the company bus every morning."

"What rubbish! I don't even wear a tie."

Zaira tugged at my shirt again. "Papa, why does that round man have one eye?"

Azaan was not to be left behind. "Papa, can you get me the 3D glasses? That will be so cool!"

"Does anyone have any questions so far?" Kriyansh spoke up again.

---

[11] Image sources: 123rf.com, Microsoft clipart

Not a single hand was raised.

"None? That's surprising. Anyway, I am sure that you are all very eager as to know as to how much will the Genius package cost? The market price for this package is Rs 2,00, 000 for one child, for one year. But for all those seated here, we have a very special deal. Can anyone take a guess?"

One hand went up this time. Mine.

Kriyansh looked in my direction. "Yes sir?"

"It's free?" I asked hopefully.

Kriyansh didn't look too happy. "No sir, it is *not* free. Anyone else? No one? Anyway, let me tell you. The special price for all those seated here is Rs 1, 00, 000. This special price is valid for a month only. If you enroll today itself, you will get another Rs 50, 000 off. In short, you will need to pay only Rs 50, 000 and save an astounding Rs 1, 50, 000 in the bargain. The tablet with pre-loaded SD card and 3D glasses will be provided by Genius Education, absolutely free of cost. "

I could see Ayesha's almond eyes lit up as she remarked, "That's really cheap, isn't it Burhan?"

"Hello, there's no way I am falling for this one. I thought we came here for a certificate and a dinner?"

"Yes, but we can keep an open mind, no? If Genius has over 250, 000 students, then they must be doing something right? It's only a matter of Rs 50, 000."

"Only? *Only?* Madam, that amount is my monthly gross salary, that too without tax deductions!"

"You shouldn't be stingy. After all, it is a matter of Azaan's future."

I was affronted by the harsh words and cursed myself for coming to this accursed place. "*I am being stingy?* How can you say that? You are always accusing me of blowing up money and now suddenly I am stingy?"

"I am in no mood to fight with you right now. Just think, Burhan! We will be saving Rs 1, 50, 000. That's two free trips to Europe!"

I scratched my head trying to figure out what was going on. Ayesha was technically correct, yet something didn't feel right. The whole ambience was beginning to feel claustrophobic.

Kriyansh was not done yet. "The tablet will be preloaded with 500 free movies, both Hindi and English, which can only be accessed by a password. Parents can watch these movies when their child is not studying. If you were to buy these movie DVDs in the market, they alone would cost you more than Rs 50, 000. In addition, the tablet is pre-loaded with Skype and WhatsApp so that you can make unlimited free calls and messages over internet. Now, where can you find a better deal than this? The bag of goodies doesn't end here. All those enrolling today will be getting a free buffet dinner coupon for parents and children at Taja Hotel, a three star hotel at Ghatkopar with five star gastronomic delights, worth Rs 10, 000. In essence, you will be more than recovering your cost the moment you pay for the Genius package."

Great! Now he has managed to confuse me thoroughly. I looked at Ayesha; she seemed to be mesmerized by the wily Sindhi.

"I would like to end my speech by an appeal to all parents to apply their minds and think. Would you send your child to an expensive tuition class when he/she can learn from the comfort of your home, under your watchful eyes?

"Would you invest in superficial investments like gold and property when you can invest in your child's future?"

"Would you act later when you can act now and avail of the golden opportunity?"

Ya Allah, can someone please silence this guy?

I felt distinctly uneasy as both Ayesha and Azaan looked at me with expectant eyes. We had to get out of the auditorium before the situation spiraled out of control. Lifting Zaira with my left arm and clutching Azaan's hand with my right, I stood up and made a dash for the exit.

"What are you doing?" Ayesha yelled behind me.

"We need to leave right now."

"Why?"

"We must get ice cream for Zaira before the shops close."

Ayesha protested vehemently, but I marched ahead.

A polite applause broke out through the auditorium, signaling the end of Kriyansh's spiel. Danielle retook the mike from Kriyansh.

"Thank you, sir, for that hugely motivational speech. I am sure everyone here is eager to enroll their child today itself, for the Genius program. Aren't you, parents and children? Say it aloud. Louder, everyone....louder, louder."

What's her problem? Had she gone deaf? Clearly, I had made a monumental mistake in appraising Danielle, my liking for her dropped multiple notches.

"All the children are requested to gather backstage wherein their names will be called out one by one to come on stage. Mr Kriyansh will personally handover a certificate, a medal, and two discount coupons of Rs 1, 00, 000 and Rs 50, 000 respectively. Once the felicitation is over, please remember to hand over the duly filled discount forms to a volunteer nearest to you and collect a coupon for tea and snacks."

We had reached the exit. *A few more steps and we would be out.* Unfortunately, an overweight security guard blocked our path out of the blue.

"Sorry sir. This exit is closed."

"What do you mean by this exit is closed? "

"If you wish to exit, you will need to go the doorway at the opposite end of the auditorium."

"Boss, this is an emergency. I need to go to the washroom."

"Sorry sir, rules are rules."

It was at that very moment, Danielle delivered the coup d'état.

"For those parents still wondering what to do and how to do, Genius is making an add-on offer that will blow your mind. Genius will offer a free trial period of one month. Those interested in continuing after the trial period, will have the option of converting the payment into an EMI at 0% interest."

An event volunteer came running up to me, breathless. "Sir, you may please join us for snacks and beverages before you leave."

My antennas became instantly alert. "Why this generosity all of a sudden? Listen buster, we are not interested in signing up. So you can keep your snacks to yourself."

The volunteer looked a trifle confused as he offered me a few event coupons. "Sir, these coupons are yours. I cannot keep them."

"Why are you trying to force these coupons upon us?"

"Sir, that lady over there asked me to give them to you."

I looked at the direction of the volunteer's outstretched hand and spotted Ayesha. She was busy munching on a samosa and some chips from a paper tray.

I looked at the coupons closely. There were three identical coupons for snacks and tea. The fourth coupon was a dinner invitation to Taja hotel, Ghatkopar. I looked at Ayesha again. She was waving out to me and beckoning me to join her. I glared at the volunteer who was smiling at me patronizingly.

"You have made the right decision. Welcome to the Genius family, sir. "

Expectations

"Ask Muthuswamy Nair to meet me!" bellowed the People's Bank branch manager Bunty Singh to the office boy, Nilesh.

"Sir, you mean Muthuswamy Aiyyar," corrected Nilesh.

"Oye, Aiyyar or Nair, *ki farak painda*? All South Indian names sound the same. Now stop wasting time and ask him to meet me." Nilesh, who was a staunch *Rajinikanth* devotee, wanted to differ with the branch boss, but prudence prevailed.

Bunty Singh was a contradiction of sorts. At first sight, he appeared to be the quintessential strapping *sardar* sporting a turban, *kara, and* even a *kirpan,* with a larger than life image. But beneath the layers, Bunty Singh had no qualms in tweaking tradition at the altar of convenience. His hair was always cropped short and he preferred to be clean shaven, creating some confusion in his social and professional circles. Bunty Singh never hesitated to speak his mind and let others know who was the boss. Like his relatives who had entrepreneurship in their DNA, Bunty too wanted to either own a vehicle parts business or open a restaurant. The inflection point came during graduation when Bunty obtained healthy grades, much to his own surprise and against general expectations, creating a state of confusion and indecisiveness. In the turmoil that followed, Bunty finally opted for a corporate career in the banking industry, and didn't look back ever since, except when his father, mother, brother, wife, brother-in-law, brother-in-law's parents, servant, driver pointed out that perhaps a business would have been a more suitable career option.

Muthuswamy Aiyyar was People Bank's pillar of strength and its most cherished employee. Short, diminutive, not blessed with great looks (conventional or otherwise), Muthuswamy was a creature of tradition, habit and discipline. His daily routine was a set menu, starting with waking up at 6 a.m. sharp, followed by puja, then yoga, breakfast at 8 a.m., office by 9 a.m., home by 6 p.m., dinner by 7 p.m., news at 7.30 p.m., hitting the bed at 10 p.m. Muthuswamy's dream was to get a government job, which was fulfilled when he got an appointment letter from People's Bank. Being promoted from senior clerk to junior credit officer a year ago was the icing on the cake. Muthuswamy had only one primary ambition in life now that occupied his very being 24x7, as he stood face to face with his boss who was perusing a thick file.

"Oye Muthu, what are you doing here? Did you need something?" asked Bunty Singh.

"Sir, you asked me to meet you, remember?"

"Ah, yes, yes." Bunty Singh scratched his forehead and after a pause continued, "Oye Muthu, what is going on?" Bunty Singh tried to adopt the softest tone possible, in order to avoid offending his best employee.

Muthuswamy blinked his eyes, not being able to comprehend his boss's hint. Bunty Singh decided to go back to his tried and tested blunt approach.

"Yaar, why are you a *dukhi aatma* these days? I am getting a lot of complaints from your department. One of our loyal customers,

Mr Sudip Dasgupta, came up to me the other day saying that we have declared him a willful defaulter."

"So?"

"So, the only problem is that Mr Sudip has never taken a loan from this bank."

"Sir, mistakes happen once in a while. We are human after all," said Muthuswamy defiantly.

"Accha? And what about Mr Vikas Chourasia, our premium customer, who wanted a loan of one crore? He is very agitated."

"Sir, we gave him the loan, *na*? What is he still cribbing about, *huh*?" Muthuswamy muttered.

"*Shree* Muthuswamy Aiyyar, I wish that were the case. In fact you gave the loan and credited the amount to Mrs Laxmi Zaveri's account, who is not very happy either," sighed Bunty.

"Hmmmm."

Bunty Singh gaped at Muthuswamy for a few seconds and then asked "Hmmmm? That's all you have got to say? Hmmmm?"

"Sir, what else to say now? I will reverse the transaction immediately. No big deal."

"And then we have a new customer Mr Devendra Pathak, who complained that we have opened his bank account twice and that he has been levied penalty for not maintaining minimum balance."

"Hmmmm."

"There we go again. Muthu, are you alright? And why have you worn your boxing gloves for this meeting? Here I am trying to explain what has gone wrong, but you don't want to accept your mistakes. Remember Muthu, I am your boss."

"How can I forget, sir? You remind us day and night," replied a belligerent Muthuswamy.

Bunty Singh thought hard as to how to get a handle on his most valued employee. Had it been any other employee, he would have no hesitation in kicking such a fellow out of the branch. But the same stance could not be applied for the employee who did bulk of the grunt work for the branch. Not immediately anyway.

Bunty Singh tried his fatherly figure formula. "Muthu, of late, I can't help noticing that you are remaining withdrawn and absent minded." Bunty Singh had taken a shot in the dark, but Muthuswamy didn't respond.

"Is everything okay with you? Is there any way I can help you?"

"Sir, thank you for your concern, but I am not in the mood right now. I want to take a few days off, starting today," said Muthuswamy bluntly.

For a brief moment, Bunty was tempted to hurl a few expletives and slap Muthuswamy. Instead, he replied with a huge fake smile, "No problem. You want leave? Take it. I want my old Muthu back as soon as possible."

Muthuswamy left his boss's cabin without so much as a word of thanks. Bunty Singh felt like flinging his paper stopper at Muthuswamy's turned back. Instead, he called his favourite office informer into his cabin.

"Jeev Abraham reporting sir."

"I can see that. And you can stop saluting me. This is not the army."

"Sorry sir."

Bunty Singh looked at Jeev Abraham closely. All of twenty-three years, medium height and built, sporting machine cropped hair, Jeev's ambition was to become the favourite subordinate of Bunty Singh, an honour that Bunty Singh had unofficially accorded to over two dozen staff members in People's branch.

"I have a job for you, Jeev."

"Thank you very much, sir. I will satisfy you completely, sir."

Bunty Singh shook his head exasperatedly. "Can you first listen to what I have to say?"

"Sorry sir."

"This Muthuswamy fellow is acting all strange these days. Bugger won't tell me what his problem is and we are getting a lot of complaints."

"Okay sir."

"No, it's not okay. Listen, he is a South Indian and so are you. Can you talk to him in your local language and try and understand what his problem is?"

"But sir, he is from Chennai and I am from Kerala."

"This is exactly why our country is not making progress; each one thinking about their own city only. Both of you are from South India, no?"

"Yes sir, you are right, sir. I will get all the facts and figures and report back to you, sir. Thank you for this esteemed opportunity, sir."

Bunty Singh sighed and waved Jeev away.

Barely a couple of hours later, Bunty received a call on his cell phone. It was Jeev.

"You got back very quickly. Do you have some news?" Bunty asked excitedly.

"*Err* no, boss, dialed your number by mistake. You see, your number is the first on my scrolling—"

Bunty's excitement switched to irritation immediately as he disconnected the call abruptly.

Jeev's name flashed on Bunty's cellphone again after one hour.

"Yes Jeev?" asked Bunty, in a less than gentle tone.

"Very sorry, sir. This stupid phone is driving me crazy. I don't know how, but it dialed your number by mistake again."

"Why the hell don't you throw out the damn phone and buy a new one?" screamed Bunty exasperatedly. *Bloody duffer.*

The same evening, Bunty received a third call from Jeev. This time, Bunty gave him a mouthful.

"*&%$#@^&*!%$#@%%$**"

"Sir, sir, I have spoken to Muthuswamy."

A surprised Bunty stopped swearing. "Oh, why didn't you tell me earlier? What did he say?"

"It seems that Muthuswamy's son has goofed up in his exams big time. The entire family is very upset."

"*Oh teri!* Is that it? Such a minor issue. Is Muthu at home right now? "

"I think so, sir."

"*Ek kaam karte hain.* Let's pay him a quick visit. I know how to cheer him up."

"Okay, sir."

Bunty Singh disconnected the call and informed his secretary that he would be out of office for a couple of hours.

●

Bunty Singh and Jeev Abraham were soon standing at the doorstep of Muthuswamy's house. A name plate reading 'Muthuswamy Aiyyar & Meena Aiyyar' was affixed on the door. Bunty Singh rang the doorbell. An elegant looking lady in her early thirties opened the door. She had a lean frame, more than average height and looked resplendent in a green silk saree.

Jeev made the introduction."We are from the bank, ma'am."

"Sorry, but we are not interested," replied the lady, as she proceeded to shut the door.

A surprised Bunty rang the door bell again. The lady opened the door with a frown.

"Ma'am, there is a misunderstanding. We are from People's Bank. I am the branch manager, Bunty Singh and this is my associate Jeev Abraham. Muthu is our colleague."

"Muthu?"

"Sorry, I mean Muthuswamy."

"Uh, huh."

"Who is it, Meena?" It was Muthuswamy, he had joined his wife at the door. Bunty Singh had difficulty imagining the duo as a couple.

"Aah, Sir!" exclaimed Muthuswamy, surprised with the unexpected visitors. "What brings you here?"

"We were just passing by your house and thought that we would drop in to see you."

"Hmmmm."

"Aren't you going to invite us into your house?"

"Oh, all right," said Muthuswamy reluctantly.

Bunty and Jeev had taken a few steps into the house when Muthuswamy stopped them.

"I am sorry, sir. Both of you will need to take off your shoes."

Bunty Singh gritted his teeth, but obeyed Muthuswamy, thanking his stars that he didn't have any holes in his socks as he removed his shoes.

Muthuswamy's house was spartan and understated. It had traditional furniture, neatly stacked and well spaced out. The flooring had old fashioned mosaic tiles, while the walls had been freshly painted with soft lemony yellow. A huge book rack stuffed with various genres of books was placed alongside the largest wall. A series of dancing wooden statuettes adorned the four corners of the hall. Fragrance of freshly burnt incense sticks permeated the room. Bunty Singh hated the smell.

As Bunty was being led into the hall along with Jeev, he noticed that there were five persons seated in the hall. On one sofa, there was an elderly, balding, dark-complexioned gentleman seated beside a fair-complexioned, plumpish lady with jet black, oiled hair embroidered with Jasmine flowers.

"That is my father-in-law and mother-in-law," Muthuswamy said.

On the other sofa, a young lady bedecked in jewellery and Muthuswamy's doppelganger were seated.

"That is my brother and his wife."

A morose looking teenager, with facial hair and pimples sprouting uniformly across his face was seated at the far corner. The unhappy boy stood out like a sore thumb.

"Why are the men so dark and the women so fair in this house?" asked Jeev, out of the blue. He had been unusually quiet till now. Though a similar query was playing on Bunty Singh's mind, he glared at Jeev and motioned him to shut up.

"Is that boy your son?" Bunty Singh asked, pointing to the teenager.

Muthuswamy replied with a look of disgust. "Unfortunately, yes. I am ashamed to call him my son."

Bunty Singh was taken aback. *"Oh teri!* Why?"

"We had great expectations from him. It was our dream that he excels in studies and gets a good job in a government company."

"You mean you wanted him to become someone like me?"

Muthuswamy paused and replied, "Not exactly, we wanted something much better for him. But now, it's all over."

"I did the best I could, *Appa*. But I told you so many times that I am not interested in doing a job, I want to start my own business," stated the boy defiantly.

Muthuswamy sighed and declared to his wife, "Meena amma, not only is your son a duffer, he is also a moron."

"Muthuswamy sir, I think duffer and moron mean the same thing," observed Jeev.

Bunty Singh looked daggers at Jeev and hissed. "Please offer your opinion only when asked."

Meena Aiyyar lost her composure and began to wail. "This is the fault of our *'karma'*. I said so many times that we should go to Murugan temple and do a puja, but is there anyone who will listen to me in this house?"

"Murugan temple is good, but you should have gone to the Ayappa temple instead. I hear that chances of getting one's wishes fulfilled are higher in Ayappa temple," commented Meena Aiyyar's mother (*jasmine lady*).

Meena Aiyyar's father interjected, "*Naansense*. Look at me. I didn't become successful by visiting temples. You want to know my secret?"

"*Aiyyo*, what success, *huh*?" interrupted the jasmine lady.

"Can you allow me to complete what I am saying for once, Revati?"

While the jasmine lady sulked, the old man continued, "What was I saying? Damn, I forgot."

"You were going to tell us some secret, Appa," Meena Aiyyar reminded him.

"*A-haan*, the secret. Do you want to know how I have kept my brain and memory sharp for all these years? Tell me, tell me huh? Okay, I will tell you. One word – *chyavanprash*. One spoon in the morning after waking up and one spoon in the night before going to sleep."

"But *Tatta*, I hate chyavanprash. It tastes like cow dung."

"*Naansense*. Have you tasted cow dung, kid? You should pay heed to my years of wisdom and knowledge."

"*Aiyyo*, ignore the old man. You should be visiting temples. First make God happy, everything else will automatically be taken care of," his wife declared with an air of finality.

"Everyone is getting this all wrong. The real fault lies with today's technology. TV, video games, social media, instant gratification. When will the kids study? The kids today don't know the meaning of hard work, they get everything so easily. You should have seen how hard we studied during our school days. Study time meant study time, no time pass," Muthuswamy's twin brother said.

"Please don't brag, you failed twice in your matriculate exam," the young jewellery lady interjected.

"Parvati!" screamed the brother.

"Actually there are a number of reasons," Muthuswamy said, with the mannerism of a professor lecturing his students. "First, the terrible handwriting. I mean, the boy himself has difficulty understanding what he writes, forget about others. We hoped that that the boy would perhaps show interest in medicine, which would justify his handwriting. Wrong! I had also arranged for his admission into Kota coaching classes with great difficulty. But the boy kept cribbing that he would not get home made food and his mom supported him. Maybe, I should have sent both of them to Kota together."

Bunty Singh walked up to Muthuswamy and announced in a low tone of voice. "I think I can help your son. Can I speak to him?"

Muthuswamy looked at Bunty Singh with a hint of suspicion. "What do you want to tell him?"

"He needs motivation. I will give him a motivational speech. After all, as a leader, that's what I do best, giving motivational speeches."

Muthuswamy was not convinced. "How will that help? Have we not given him enough motivation all these years?"

Bunty forced a smile and patted Muthuswamy on the shoulder. "*O yaara*, let me try?"

He walked up to the boy and asked, "Hello my boy, what is your name?"

The boy did not respond or even acknowledge Bunty Singh's presence. Bunty tried again.

"Ahem, what is your name, *puttar?*"

"Krishnaswamy Aiyyar, not *puttar*," said the boy coldly.

"*Oye teri! Itna gussa?* Do you know who I am?"

"No."

"Listen, I am your father's boss. I want to tell you something."

"I am not in the mood right now. Can you tell my father instead?"

Teri ma di...Like father, like son. Deserves a kick on his butt. Arrogant idiot.

"But I still want to tell you. Hear me out." Bunty Singh took a pause before continuing, "Try and try until you succeed. Failures are steps of the ladder to success. Albert Einstein famously said that 'I have not failed, I have just found 10, 000 ways that won't work'."

"Actually, that was Thomas Edison."

"*Ki farak painda*? It's not important who said it, the message is the key. If you don't do well in studies, so what? Life is so much bigger than studies."

There were surprised looks across the room. Muthuswamy and family were flabbergasted with what they had just heard. Bunty Singh had just committed blasphemy.

Krishnaswamy's face brightened up. "That is exactly what I have been trying to tell everyone here. Famous people like Mark Zuckerberg, Steve Jobs, Bill Gates were all college dropouts. I too want to start my business and become famous one day."

A horrified Muthuswamy cautioned Bunty from speaking further. "Sir, I don't think your motivational speech is helping. Let us handle this problem our way instead of complicating matters."

Jeev tapped Bunty Singh's shoulders again and whispered, "Sir, I really think we should leave now."

"*Theek hai, theek hai*. Okay, all the best, Krishnaswamy. Okay bye, Muthu, bye Mrs Muthu."

"Sir, Muthuswamy, not Muthu," Jeev whispered, trying to correct Bunty.

"Oye, chup kar, oye," Bunty hissed back.

Bunty and Jeev left hurriedly, with no attempt from Muthuswamy and family to hold them back.

Once out of the house, Bunty realized that he had forgotten something. "Do you know what the kid's score in the exam was?"

"No sir, but I took some pictures of the report card lying on the side table with my smart phone."

"*Shabaash*, Jeev. Let me see the pictures."

Jeev handed the smart phone promptly to Bunty.

"Oye, these pictures are all hazy; can't make out anything. Wait; there is one decent picture here."

Bunty Singh turned to the most recent picture and almost did a double take. He raised his fist angrily at Muthuswamy's house and shouted, "*Teri &^%$... Teri &^%$#.*Bloody psychos, lunatics, maniacs!"

"What is the problem, sir?"

Jeev Abraham looked at the picture on his mobile phone and squinted his eyes.

"Enlarge the picture, you idiot."

Jeev enlarged the picture. There was a figure written in bold at the bottom of the card, encircled in blank ink.

'97.5%.'

Faceoff

The night was chilly and the streets desolate. It was well past midnight, with a few cars on the road. We were returning from a boisterous party with close friends at a popular city restaurant. The window glasses of our car were rolled up; the vehicle heater had made the interior warm and cozy. The vehicle stereo was belting out mellifluous Ariana Grande hits. Aided by the generous doses of alcohol content (*one complete glass of mild beer*), I was getting into the mood and made a couple of subtle moves.

"Stop it Dev, you are distracting me," Avantika chided me.

"*Tch… tch…* That's your problem, Avu. You barred me from taking the wheel. I am simply exercising my rights as your co-passenger and boyfriend. Can you try and focus on the road please?"

"Rights, my foot. This is so unfair! You are exploiting the situation."

"Of course, my dear. I plead guilty."

I slid my right hand further up Avantika's skirt, attempting to get a feel of the silky smoothness of her skin and tease her inner thighs with my fingers.

"What's this, eh?" My fingers had encountered a tough thick material below Avantika's skirt, which prevented further access.

"That is my anti pervert *kavach,*" Avantika chuckled.

"Ha ha, very funny," I replied sarcastically.

I tried hard, but found it very difficult to slide my hand beneath the thick material. *Did they make undergarments from Teflon these days?* I was not going to give up so easily. I clasped Avantika's waist and gradually inched my fingers upwards towards other erogenous zones on her body like ear lobes. I massaged her ear lobes and then poked my finger into her ear's passage. *(It didn't go in of course, my index finger was much bigger).*

Avantika's head sprung away. "No, Dev. You are tickling me!"

I tried again, this time placing my hand on Avantika's back. She was wearing a low cut, noodle strapped blouse, making my imagination run wild. I began to run my fingers up and down her back, massaging her periodically and making a mental note of the number of knots that required to be untied *(it was a pretty large number).*

Wtf! There was not an iota of response or bodily signal from Avantika; I might as well have been massaging a block of wood. *Were my fingers losing their magic?* In other circumstances, all I had to do was simply wriggle my fingers in front of her, to unlock the gates of passion.

Avantika sensed my thoughts and looked in my direction, her eyes smiling mischievously. "Patience, my dear. We will be home soon—"

I looked at the speedometer, the needle was hovering at 20 km/hr. I realized that the speedometer was not lying, when I saw a couple of auto rickshaws and a BEST bus overtake us with little effort *(non stop honking)*[12]. We were still fifteen kilometers away from home and

---

[12]   Avantika was learning to drive. No further comment.

mental calculations indicated that we would *definitely not be home soon*. I was desperate for action. Quick action.

I swiveled the upper half of my body in Avantika's direction and lunged forward to plant a slew of kisses on Avantika's sexy back.

Screeeeech.

Avu had pressed the brakes at a very inopportune moment. I lost my balance, and my open mouth made contact with the hard steering wheel, instead of Avantika's back.

"Oh my god, are you hurt?"

"Why the sudden brake?" I castigated Avantika.

"Red light signal," she replied calmly.

"So what?"

"And traffic cop hiding behind that signal."

I looked to the side and saw a traffic cop running towards our car. *What was the cop doing at this unearthly hour?*

The cop tapped his baton on our car window and asked us to roll down our windows. He was wearing a neatly pressed white shirt over khaki trousers and the trademark blue woolen cap. No sooner had we rolled down our windows, a breathalyzer was stuffed into my mouth. The results were not good.

The cop smiled at me and remarked, "Drinking, huh?"

"Yes sir. But I am not driving."

"Okay, okay. What about her?" the cop asked me, pointing the breathalyzer in Avantika's direction.

"Don't even think about it. I am not putting that filthy contraption in my mouth," Avantika thundered.

Avantika's tone scared off the cop, but he was not about to allow his night prowl go empty handed. Taking a good look inside the car and then at me, he remarked, "Why are you not wearing your seat belt?"

"Yes, I also tell him so many times, but Dev never wears his seat belt. You should give him a real scolding, sir." Avantika sided with the surprised and confused cop.

"Yes, yes. Listen to ma'am. Always wear your seat belt, mister."

"Thank you sir. Do you want to check my license? Or shall we go now?" Avantika offered, fluttering her eyelashes more than necessary.

"Err…you can go," said the baffled cop, muttering under his breath, before walking away.

"Finally," I exclaimed in relief, rolling up the windows again. The mouth injury and the interruption by the cop had not dimmed my spirit, as I looked at Avantika with love and longing *(and some lust).*

Avantika switched on the ignition, but she did not put the car into motion. She looked at me and read my mind, understanding the gravity of the situation. Taking pity on me, Avantika took my hands and wrapped them around her slender waist. She then enveloped her arms around me. Her mouth was now tantalizingly close to mine, as we looked deep into each other's eyes. My heart was beating rapidly, in anticipation of tasting those luscious lips.

Tap, tap.

Someone was knocking at our car window again. I cursed, as Avantika had loosened her grip, and I was forced to open my eyes.

It was a scrawny little boy, barely seven to eight years of age, semi-naked, with unkempt auburn hair. Covered in grime and sporting flimsy nylon shorts, the boy placed his sooty hands on our car window and peered into our car, exploring the contents with his eyes. Not exactly thrilled at having a beggar boy invading my moment, I wanted to shoo him away. But the possible erosion of my carefully cultivated image in Avantika's eyes, restrained me. Avantika was looking at me intently, while I pretended to rummage my trouser pockets for change.

After a couple of minutes I declared, "Sorry Avu, can't seem to find any change. But we shouldn't be encouraging these beggars anyway by giving them money. These fellows are like lazy leeches. Why can't they work for a living? Like they say, you should teach a man how to fish instead of giving him fish."

Avantika put up her hand up to stop me and then opened her own purse. Suddenly, a huge pair of paws descended from nowhere on the car window. They belonged to an ugly stray mongrel, who seemed to be looking at me with suspicion.

"Aww, how cute!" Avantika remarked.

I disagreed with Avantika, glad that the windows were rolled up, but kept my opinion to myself. The creature was hanging his long tongue out of his mouth repeatedly, as if he had swallowed a red chili. His teeth were not very healthy; they inspired fear of the fourteen injections.

Encouraged by Avantika's reactions, the boy made a pitiful face, and began to gesture repeatedly for a handout. Avantika promptly took out a hundred rupee note from her purse and asked me to hand over the note to the boy. The boy's eyes almost doubled in anticipation.

I couldn't bear to see hard earned money being thrown away like this, so I placed the note back in Avantika's purse, to her consternation.

To pacify Avantika, I pretended to search my pockets again and this time, I extracted a ten rupee note, despite my efforts to locate one and two rupee coins. I rolled down my window and reluctantly handed over the note to the kid. The fellow's greed was not satiated and he continued to pester for more.

"C'mon Dev, they look so hungry. Don't you have some food in this car?" asked Avantika.

I didn't know why Avantika wanted to compete with Mother Teresa, but it was a good idea. I put my hand into my food stocks kept in the rear pockets of the car seats. Deftly sorting away the apples and dry fruits and hiding them securely, I took out a half open packet of mouldy glucose biscuits along with damp *samosas* and handed them over to the boy.

I declared grandly, "Today is your lucky day, kid. And don't hog everything; keep some biscuits for that dog of yours also."

There, killing four birds with one stone: disposal of leftovers, Swacch Bharat, good deed and impressing girlfriend.

The dog started sniffing the food in the boy's hands and then suddenly leapt onto my side of the window again, placing his terrifying paws just over the glass edge. The mangy monster threw a dirty look at me and then without warning, he started howling. *The ingrate.* Petrified, I began to roll up the windows.

The next instant, I found myself standing outside my car. Avantika was still on the driving wheel, but there was a stranger seated next to her. Clueless as to what had just happened, I tried to get a good look at the stranger, but the car had begun to move away. As the car collected speed, I tried to run behind it but stumbled and fell. In desperation, I called out Avantika's name.

"Woof, woof, woof, woof, woof."

Something was wrong, very wrong. I tried again. *"Woof, woof, woof, woof, woof."*

Had I gone mad? Or was it some bad dream? I tried to pinch myself, but couldn't. I looked at my hands. They were gone, replaced by paws. My body was stinking. I felt that I had not taken a bath in years; I felt like scratching most of my body parts, especially the region behind my ears. My head was in a tizzy, the world was spinning around me.

"Hungry, Shaktiman?" It was a child's voice. I looked up. It was the scrawny beggar kid. I looked around for Shaktiman, there was no one besides me. The boy was looking straight at me.

"Let's have dinner, Shaktiman," said the boy, as he sat down on the pavement and beckoned me to sit along with him.

Who Shaktiman, what Shaktiman? Why was this fellow calling me Shaktiman?

"Woof, woof, woof, woof, woof," I replied angrily. No, this did not sound right. I tried again. *"Woof, woof, woof, woof, woof."*

The boy placed his little hand on my head reassuringly. "Come here," said the kid, picking up a discarded newspaper from the road, and spreading it on the pavement. Thereafter, he opened a torn plastic bag and laid out the food contents across the newspaper.

"Our feast for tonight," the boy said to me, smiling. There were a few stale pieces of bread, the familiar damp samosas, and the mouldy glucose biscuits. My hunger pangs were assaulted by the sight of this sorry excuse of a meal, not fit for even a dog.

All of a sudden, three raucous youngsters squeezed tightly onto a ramshackle moped, braked their two wheeler loudly in front of us. The moped driver was a hybrid between a boy and a man, of uneven proportions; triangular faced with king sized beard, heavily built arms and chest, narrow waist, eucalyptus tree like legs. The fellow seated third, was clean shaven with a roundish face, double breasted with nipples jutting out from his t-shirt, generous portions of stomach and butt mirroring one another. Half of the guy's butt extended beyond the rear of the moped and rested on thin air, unbalancing the poor moped, which appeared to be in a takeoff position. The youngster had his hands full with three beer bottles and a freshly baked aromatic pizza. Sandwiched in between these two characters, was a square-faced teenage girl with crew cut hair, sporting a bandana and even physical proportions (*one could draw two narrow straight lines running from her top to her bottom*). The sandwiched girl was holding a battery operated CD player, playing terrifying musical sounds at peak volume. All three sported expansive tattoos of undecipherable text codes on their forearms (*the trio may have got a heavily discounted bulk deal*).

"Why did you stop?" asked a feminine voice. It was the guy seated third.

"I want to *pee*, either of you care to join me?" the first guy said.

"I'll go too," said a second female voice. It was the sandwiched girl; she had switched off the CD player. *Thank God*.

"I can't figure out if I want to go, but I will give it a try," said the third guy.

"No Rams, you have got to stay here with our stuff," the girl stated firmly.

"And don't guzzle all the beer behind our backs. We will be watching you."

"Bugger off, Viks." The trio got off their moped painstakingly, one by one.

"Let's do it right here, in the middle of the road," said the girl with a daring smile on her face.

"Don't be silly, Paddy. If anyone catches us, especially a cop, we could land into trouble." It was 'Rams', the double breasted guy.

"Chicken? *Puck puck puckak puck,*" taunted the girl.

"No way," declared 'Rams', as he kept the goodies on the road, unzipped his trouser with his grubby fingers, lowered his trousers clumsily and got down to business. It was not a pleasant sight for the faint hearted. His two accomplices cheered and clapped from the sidelines.

After struggling for a couple of minutes with sporadic infrequent droplets, 'Rams' upped his trousers and zipped it back. "Done, both your turns now," he declared.

I was distracted by the tantalizing fragrance of the pizza and the sight of the beer bottle, lying unattended on the road. I was wondering how to get my hands (*sorry, paws*) on the pizza and beer.

Before the bearded hybrid 'Viks' and the gaunt 'Paddy' could do their 'thing', my self-proclaimed kid companion, who had already sensed the opportunity, walked up to the trio, and commenced his skillful 'I am very hungry, can you feed me?' gesturing act.

The girl looked at the kid intensely and then mimicked him. "*Can you give me some money, sir? I am very hungry and have not eaten anything for days.*" 'Viks' and 'Rams' burst into laughter, much to the beggar kid's bewilderment.

"You can be mean, Paddy," 'Viks' commented, still laughing. "Listen kid, we can give you some beer," Viks told the kid, winking serially at 'Paddy' and 'Rams'.

Aaah, I thought they would never ask. My newly acquired tail was wagging itself automatically without my permission. I wanted to say *Yes, yes, yes.* Instead, I could feel my tongue salivating and moving in and out of my mouth rapidly.

But what did the kid say? "No sir." Just like that. *Silly boy.* He pointed to the pizza box lying on the road.

"You want Pizza, *huh*? Sorry boy, you will have to earn it. Drink this beer and then you get a slice," said 'Viks' definitively, his winking to the other two more pronounced than ever.

To supplement the kid's efforts, I decided to make an appeal of my own. Walking on all fours was becoming frustrating, so I stood up on my hind legs, tried to balance myself and walked up to the trio gingerly. I tried to say something.

"Woof, woof, woof, woof, woof." It was of no use, &*%$* %$#**!

The girl looked at me with disgust and asked the kid, "Does this ugly animal belong to you?"

*Who was this *&^%*% calling ugly? And hello, I don't 'belong' to anyone.*

"Yes, he is my best friend, Shaktiman," replied the kid.

"Oho, you mean like Superman, Batman, Shaktiman, eh?" remarked El Fatso 'Rams' generating a fresh round of laughter amongst themselves. I felt like sinking my teeth into all three of them.

"Can this Shaktiman of yours do any tricks?" asked the girl.

"Yes, he is the *bestest* dog in the whole world, he knows everything," replied the kid stupidly. This was one confused kid or surely a number one *pheku*.

"I will show you some of his tricks," said the kid confidently. He then looked into my eyes and instructed, "Shaktiman, do namaste."

I looked at the kid and then the trio and back again at the kid, but did nothing. Trying to balance myself on two legs was bad enough, I wasn't going to try to do a namaste.

The kid tried again. "Shaktiman, do namaste." I just sat there and did nothing.

The kid did not give up. "I taught him the namaste a few days back, maybe he has forgotten. But he is an expert on the reverse flip. Shaktiman, show them the reverse flip."

Reverse flip, ha. You think I am a circus clown? Keep fantasizing kiddo. The kid patted my head gently and again, "Shaktiman, do the reverse flip. C'mon, you can do it."

"What a fraud!" remarked El Fatso.

"And so bloody lazy. We will give you and your dog a last chance. Rams, throw a slice of pizza as far as you can. Let's see if this dog can fetch," said the bearded hybrid.

El Fatso was alarmed. "No way, man. I am not throwing away a perfectly good slice for this mongrel. You want a show, you sacrifice your slice."

The girl lost her patience, took out a pizza slice from the box, threw it afar and ordered, "Fetch."

Before I could react, the kid had already started running towards the fallen pizza slice, taking all of us by surprise. I recovered the quickest and noticed that they were absorbed in watching the kid. It was a split second decision. I took the opportunity in both jaws. Clasping the pizza box within my teeth, I made a dash in the opposite direction. This time, my tail automatically came between my legs.

El Fatso saw me first. "Hey, the dog is running away with our pizza. Stop him! Thief, thief!"

"Throw something at him for god's sake to stop him, instead of simply shouting," the girl screeched frantically.

El Fatso looked around and said, "I can throw a beer bottle at him, but I will need to finish the beer before that."

"*Sheesh*, duffer. Find some stones," the girl yelled. My kid companion had returned by then, empty-handed and was pleading with them not to hurt me.

I was gaining distance. A second later, I could hear stones being flung in my direction, but I was almost out of harm's way now, with my booty. Thankfully, it occurred to none of the three, to chase me on their moped.

Huffing and puffing with all the running, I had to stop, when I had difficulty breathing. I was out of sight now, as I happily opened the box and eyed the contents greedily. Ravenous, I was about to sink my teeth into the delicacy, when guilt pieced my heart. I had forgotten all about the kid until now. *&%$@**/%. How could I enjoy my meal knowing that the kid was hungry? Well, he did have one slice with him, or did he? *I couldn't remember seeing anything in his little hands, when he had returned.*

All of a sudden, I heard angry growling sounds closing in on me. As I looked up, I saw a pair of dogs who didn't exactly look friendly, with saliva dripping from their teeth. They were eyeing both me and my meal.

"Look at the guts of this *&^%$&%, coming into our territory," the brown coloured dog appeared to be saying to the black coloured dog.

I rubbed my ears with my paws. *Was I hearing things?*

"Yeah, this foreign immigration problem is increasing day by day. Trump has a point. These fellows need to be taught a lesson," said the black coloured dog.

Great, now I could understand doggy language also. This was the pits!

"Trump who?"

"I don't know, but I heard some humans talking about him the other day."

"You are spending too much time with the humans these days! No wonder you talk all funny these days."

"What do we do with this fellow now?"

"We rip him apart and take the pizza. Smells really yummy. It has been a long time since we tasted fresh pizza with luscious chicken toppings."

"What are we waiting for? Let's charge."

My survival instinct stronger than ever, gave flight to my tired legs. Picking up my pizza box, I scampered for my life, with the two dogs in hot pursuit.

I ran in auto pilot mode and as luck would have it, I ran into my kid companion. My courage got an instant boost, as I stood behind the kid and teased my hunters. The two dogs slowed down in their tracks, unsure of their next steps and waited for the kid's reaction. The boy calmly picked up a stone from the road and waved it threateningly at the two dogs. The two dogs did not budge, daring him to carry out his threat. The boy threw the stone, and bingo, it was right on target, hitting the brown dog's torso. The dogs fled amidst howls of pain.

The danger having abated, the kid reprimanded me mildly, "Where did you run away, Shaktiman? I was looking all over for you."

I bent my head down in shame, having left my companion to fend for himself. El Beardo, El Fatso and the girl had left the place.

"Looks like you managed to get some food," said the kid, noticing the pizza box lying next to me. "Good boy Shaktiman." I beamed in pride at the words of appreciation.

We shared the pizza. Rarely had I eaten anything so delicious and satisfying in my life. The kid enjoyed each morsel, as if he were partaking in a king's feast. Seeing the kid's happiness, my own happiness increased multi-fold.

It was time to catch some sleep. The night's chill had increased and I had begun to shiver. The kid prepared a makeshift bed on the stony pavement, comprising three layers, multiple plastic packets sandwiched between two layers of old newspapers. He signaled to me to lie down next to him on this flimsy bed. I hesitated but the alternative was the cold pavement. Both of us lay down, after which, the kid produced a jute sheet from his belongings and spread it over himself and me to protect us from the cold. As I closed my eyes, the kid caressed my head affectionately.

I didn't know when I fell asleep. My sleep was broken when I felt a hand and two legs on top of me. I opened my eyes slowly and tried to move them away gently from my body. The early morning rays of the sun were beginning to make their presence felt. As I turned my head, I saw Avantika sleeping blissfully besides me. Avantika? Where was the boy? I looked at myself and saw that my human hands were back and that my tail had disappeared. *Thank god.*

Not wanting to disturb Avantika, I sprang from the bed, kissed Avantika gently on her cheeks, tiptoed out of the room and took out my car with my night clothes still on. I stopped at a local eatery to pack some freshly cooked food and drove towards the location where I had first spotted the beggar kid. When I reached the unmanned traffic signal, I saw the kid lying sprawled on the makeshift pavement bed, clutching onto the jute bag; he was still sleeping. A stray dog was patiently standing guard by his side. I tread cautiously towards the sleeping boy and placed the food packet near his head. The dog looked at me with a quizzical expression and began to wag his tail, when I patted him on his head and placed some pieces of chicken next to him. There was something very familiar about this dog, it was as if I had known him all my life.

My impromptu visit had cleared my head. I was happy about the fact that I was not going crazy after all; the entire night's episode was nothing more than a nightmare. I walked back to my car happily and switched on the ignition key. I was distracted, something didn't feel right. Switching off the ignition, I got down from the car again, and bent down to inspect the object lying next to my car.

It was an empty pizza box.

Snorefest

"**B**e relaxed and have a good night's sleep before the day of the exam," Pathak sir had advised me repeatedly.

Lying atop the top berth of the third AC compartment of the Dibrugarh-Delhi Rajdhani express, I was revisiting my strategy to crack the UPSC Prelims exam for the five hundredth and twenty-seventh time (*approximately*).

Two hours, eighty questions...should have been a piece of cake, right? One small hiccup, there were five lakh candidates vying for around 1200 vacancies every year, implying a success ratio of barely 0.24%!

It was my fifth attempt at clearing the Prelims exam, though my record at the Mains exam was much better (*I had never qualified for it and hence technically speaking, I had a superior record*). Though everyone had given up on me, including my friends and my own parents, Pathak Sir (my coaching class teacher) was the only one who recognized my passion and potential.

"The questions are a matter of luck. You need to believe in yourself, your destiny. Lady Luck *has* to smile on you some day," he would always assure me.

I had been allotted the Allahabad test centre. Allahabad station would arrive at a god forsaken time of 2.53 a.m.; the train would stop for only three minutes. I took out my mobile phone to set the alarm for 2.30 a.m. when a fleshy hand extended out of the middle berth opposite to mine and switched off the overhead lights without warning. *No basic manners, rude fellow!* Snuggling under the dusty Indian railways blanket, I closed my eyes and tried not to think about the impending exam.

"I don't want to discourage you from your dream. But how many times do you want to keep trying? Don't you think it is better to give up and get a move on?" It was dad, in an unusually friendly avatar.

I felt pity and anger for my father, a simple clerk in Shyamrao Vithaal Co-operative bank with limited dreams and vision. He would never understand my aspiration.

"*Never, I will never give up.*"

There was no way I would dare to even open my mouth in front of dad, let alone argue. *I must have been dreaming.*

Luckily for me, Pathak sir teleported himself into the scene between me and dad and began to speak in my defense.

"*Phrr... phusss...phrrrr.... phusssss....*"

"What?" dad asked, confused.

"*Phrr... phusss...phrrrr.... phusssss...*" Pathak sir repeated.

"What's that nonsense?"

"Gogol has cleared the UPSC exam, sir. I always told you that the boy is special."

The next moment, I was thrusting my fists in the air in jubilation. Magically, the UPSC passing certificate was already in my hand as I confronted my surprised dad, jabbing him with it.

"I told you I would make it. You never believed in me. What do you have to say now, eh?"

"*Phrr... phusss...phrrrr... phusssss...*" dad began to say.

"What?" It was my turn to be confused.

My surprised dad snatched the certificate from my hands, opened it and shoved it into my face. He looked disappointed.

"I knew it…Look at this, I told you."

Phrrrrrrrr…phusssssss…phrrrrrrrrrrrrr…phusssssssssss."

Pathak sir looked at the certificate, horrified. "This is impossible…Luck… *phrrrrrrr…phusssssss…* destiny… *phrrrrrrrrrrrrr…*potential…*phussssssssssss…*Prime Minister of India."

I didn't have a clue as to what dad and Pathak sir were saying. The confounded sounds they were making were getting louder and louder, acquiring a terrifying musical rhythm alternating in pitch and frequency. It seemed as if someone had thrown in some angry rattle snakes in an empty tin container and was now shaking the container.

"This is ridiculous. Will someone please do something?" asked a new unrecognizable female voice from a far off distance. I turned around, but was unable to spot anyone.

A white ethereal glow had now replaced the dark, gloomy, despondent background in my dream.

"How about throwing a bucket of water?" It was an unknown male voice.

Why can't I see these fellows? Why are they interfering in my dream?

"Where will you get a bucket here?" asked the first female voice.

"*Phrrrrrrrr…phusssssss…phrrrrrrrrrrrrr…phusssssssssss.*"

"I have had it; I am going to pull the emergency chain." An elderly sounding voice spoke up this time.

"Don't do something silly. Just tell the TC," said an elderly female voice.

"I will, but where is the damn TC?"

"Does anyone have cotton plugs?"

Too many people, too many noises in my dream. Had I entered someone else's dream by mistake?

The warm glow in the backdrop transformed into harsh white light. My dad and Pathak sir disappeared as I reluctantly rubbed my eyes open. And then I heard the terrifying noise again, even louder this time.

"*Phrrrrrrrr...phusssssss...phrrrrrrrrrrrr...phussssssssssss... phusphusphusphus...khrrrrr.*"

The source of the unearthly evil sound, emanated from a heavy duty specimen of a middle aged man, lying on his stomach on the middle berth, opposite to mine. Louder than ever, the man's snores were beating down the rattling sounds of the train as they reverberated across the various corners of the compartment. The man himself slept blissfully, whilst the compartment passengers were wide awake, darting hostile looks in the direction of the middle berth and conspiring. Various ideas on muting the raucous co-passenger were being bandied around, but willingness to take the first step was conspicuously missing. *All talk, no action!*

Now, initiative and leadership were ingrained in my DNA. Even though I didn't want to, I instinctively took the lead.

With my eyelids still partially closed, I crawled towards the steel berth rung at the side, and began to slowly get down from my berth with the agility of a circus acrobat.

"Owwww..."

"Sorry, sorry." I had stepped on someone, but not sure on whom and exactly which part of the body. As I stood on the compartment floor, my upper body shook in all directions, mirroring the train's jerks, twists and turns at full throttle. I took the support of two steel fixtures supporting the berths to prevent myself from toppling over.

I leaned forward to have a closer look at the specimen in the middle berth. Lying on his back, the guy was a heavyset creature, draped in a cream coloured silk *kurta-pyjama*. His face was covered in freckles and he sported a menacing vermillion tilak, originating from his eye brows and extending into his scalp. There was a small scar on the right cheek. He had thick fingers akin to pork sausages, each finger sporting a gold ring. *Even in his sleep, the guy appeared to give off hostile vibes.* I was beginning to have second thoughts about my mission. The good news was that the man had gone silent, all was well, we could all go back to sleep. Mission accomplished!

"*Phrrrrrrrr…phusssssss…phrrrrrrrrrrrrr…phussssssssssss… phusphusphusphus…khrrrrr.*"

The blood curdling siren went off without any warning. My nose was treated to assorted smells ranging from garlic, onion, asafoetida, sour milk and fermented rice.

Carefully measuring the area that his sweeping arm would cover, I took a step back (*precautionary measure*) and tapped the man very lightly on his shoulder.

"Excuse me, sir?"

"*Phrrrrrrrr… phusssssss… phrrrrrrrrrrrrr… phussssssssssss… phusphusphusphus… khrrrrr.*"

I stepped back to avoid the putrid blast and tapped the man again, less gently this time.

"Excuse me, sir?"

"*Phrrrrrrrr… phusssssss… phrrrrrrrrrrrrr… phussssssssssss… phusphusphusphus… khrrrrr.*"

The man was oblivious to my presence and gentle touches. I sensed my co-passengers looking at me, hoping that I would salvage the situation. I decided to take stronger measures and punched the man lightly on his shoulder before moving back two steps.

"*Excuse me, sir?*"

"*Phrrrrrrrr… phusssssss… phrrrrrrrrrrrrr… phussssssssssss… phusphusphusphus… khrrrrr.*"

In desperation, I clutched at the man's leg and began to shake him. That had the desired effect as the giant stirred from his slumber. Opening his eyes, he threw a murderous look at me. I knew it then that I had made a serious mistake.

"So sorry for having disturbed you, sir… It's uh… it's just that I, er…"

The guy's expression did not change as he waited for me to fall into the hole. *Was this guy carrying any knife or gun on the sly?* I didn't want to find out.

"I just wanted to tell you that there were some noises coming from this side…and… and…."

"And?" The giant growled.

"It's just that people were complaining, I mean… generally saying… that you might be… uh… kind of snoring. Not that anyone has a problem, but it's like middle of the night…and—"

The giant's looked at me incredulously and waved me away with his hand as if he were swatting a fly.

Pulling his blanket up, he looked at me in the eye and barked, "I DON'T SNORE."

"Yes, of course." I said in hurried agreement. It was too late; the creature had already closed his eyes and turned his face in the other direction. The conversation was now officially over.

Evading the looks of my co-passengers, I quietly climbed on to my berth again and closed my eyes. The snoring sounds had abated, much to my relief. The creature had taken cognizance of my request after all.

The speaker made the introductions, "We are honoured to have with us a very special guest, Shri Gangol Upadhay." There was a huge round of applause as my name was announced. The speaker continued, "An UPSC topper and gold medallist, Shri Gangol has been selected to be part of the special task force assisting the Prime Minister on putting development projects on the fast track. He is a youth icon, a role model and an inspiration to us all."

There was another huge round of applause. Before I could get up to speak, one of the students in the audience stood up suddenly and asked, "Sir, Indian Railways is the lifeline of India. What are your ideas to improve it?"

The speaker looked at the student sternly and reprimanded him over the microphone. "Control yourself, show some discipline."

I smiled at the speaker and motioned him to calm down. "It's okay. We must encourage our youngsters to ask questions. And this boy here has asked a pertinent question." Addressing the student directly now, I asked, "What is the most important problem facing Indian railways?"

"There are so many – safety, cleanliness, food, punctuality, seat availability."

"No, no, you have got it all wrong. The most important problem today is – snoring. Everything else is secondary."

"Snoring?"

"Yes. Do you realize how many people are affected by this phenomenon on a daily basis, train after train? "

"You are right, sir! We had never thought about it earlier."

"I know I am right. This is why the government is planning to come out with a slew of measures. First of all, snoring will be banned. Every reported instance of snoring will be liable for a fine. Second of all, every passenger will need to get their nose checked by their local doctor before getting a railway ticket. Third of all—"

A girl with spectacles raised her hand and stood up without even bothering to ask me.

"But sir, *phrrrrrrrr… phusssssss… phrrrrrrrrrrrrr… phusssssssssss.*"

I was furious. "Are you mocking me, young lady?"

"No sir, I was just *phrrrrrrrr… phusssssss… phrrrrrrrrrrrrr…*"

I woke up with a start, alarmed. *So, I must have been dreaming again!*

"*Phrrrrrrrr… phusssssss… phrrrrrrrrrrrrr… phusssssssssss… phusphusphusphus… khrrrrr.*"

I cursed (*in general*) and decided to climb down from my berth again to have a small chat with the snoring menace.

"Owwww…"

"Sorry, sorry." I seemed to have stepped on the same person again.

I stood facing the creature on the middle berth and shook his leg again. The guy's reaction was quicker this time. He turned around, sat up and rubbed his eyes. Looking at me, he raised both his hands. Alarm bells went off in my head immediately.

"Sir, I am so sorry. Please don't hit me. I am so sorry."

"Don't be melodramatic! Why would I hit you?"

"I just thought—"

"I was just stretching myself after such a good sleep."

"Oh—"

"Look, my station has arrived. Mughal sarai."

"Thank you."

"Excuse me?"

"I want to thank you; you woke me up in time."

"Oh, okay."

The man took out his luggage from underneath the lower berth, put on his shoes and got off the train without another word.

Good riddance, I thought to myself. *Now for some real sleep without interruption.* It was already 1 a.m. which meant that the train was on time and would reach Allahabad as per its scheduled time. Setting my mobile alarm at 2.30 a.m., I climbed back onto my berth and closed my eyes.

I was now standing at the United Nations assembly hall, addressing a motley of world leaders from all parts of the world – US, Russia, Australia, Saudi Arabia, Pakistan, Tanzania, etc. The US President was dressed in Arabic attire, while the Saudi Arabian prince had worn shorts and a T-shirt. *How did they allow him inside?*

The Tanzanian president was some white chap, while the Russian president was black. On second thoughts, their name plates might have got interchanged. The Pakistani prime minister was busy copying from the Australian prime minister's notes. Strangely enough, the

Indian prime minister was nowhere to be seen. What was even weirder was that I was sporting a breast plate titled 'Prime Minister'.

I put the microphone into my mouth and began to speak. "At the time of our independence, Jawarhal Nehru said and I quote, 'At the stroke of the midnight hour, when the world sleeps, India will awake to life and freedom.' Can someone please wake up the Secretary General seated on the first row? He seems to be sleeping and could fall off his chair any moment."

No one moved from their seats, the faces of the world leaders were blank. Annoyed, I stopped my address midway and walked upto the secretary general and shook him.

"Sir, please wake up."

There was a strange connection between us, my body also shook simultaneously.

"Sir, please wake up," I repeated.

"Huh?"

"Please wake up sir, we have reached...."

"Reached? What do you mean, reached? This is the United Nations office."

The United Nations office and the world leaders disappeared into thin air. I opened my eyes slowly and saw the train attendant standing next to me.

"Sir, looks like you have been dreaming. I have to collect the beddings and blankets. Please get up."

Rubbing my eyes, I asked in a groggy voice..."Uhh...have we reached Allahabad so soon? Is the train running before time? Why is the train so empty?"

"Allahabad? Sir, that was two stops ago. We have reached New Delhi station. This is the last stop."

"*Oh my god!*" I looked at my mobile; it had conked off. The battery was completely empty.

Venting my frustration on the attendant, I screamed, "Why didn't you wake me at Allahabad station, you imbecile?"

"Sir, sir, I don't know the meaning of such big words, but I know that was a bad word. Besides, I made so many loud announcements that we had reached Allahabad station."

"Don't lie on my face. If you did, then why didn't I hear you?"

Clicking his fingers, he said triumphantly, "I think sir, because you were making some very strange noises in your sleep."

"What rubbish! I never snore."

"Wait sir, I made a video on my mobile. Wait, let me show you."

Before I could protest, the guy fished out his cellphone and tapped on the video widget. I saw my own self, sleeping peacefully.

"I can't hear anything at all."

"Just a second, sir." The fellow pressed a button the side repeatedly, increasing the volume sticks. It was then I experienced my moment of truth.

"KhurRRR, Khatttara, Khattar…Khnnnnn… KhurRRR, Khatttara, Khattar… Khnnnnn… KhurRRR, Khatttara, Khattar…Khnnnnn. "

●

Epilogue

For those who are wondering as to what happened to my dream, I modified it a little and pursued a glamorous career in investment banking. I am now an investment advisor at Shyamrao Vithalrao Co-operative bank, distributing various investment literatures to the bank's customers and advising them how to fill the investment forms. In my spare time, I assist my mentor Pathak sir in running his coaching class. Morals of my story are as follows:

1. *Have a standby dream, just in case.*
2. *Always have cotton plugs handy, when travelling in trains.*
3. *Keep the mobile phone charged at all times*
4. *Never trust the train attendant.*

Memory Bytes

I was seated on the fifth row, at a corner of the large college auditorium, along with my friend, Vanita Puri. We were discussing the finer points of the annual award ceremony for academic excellence, focusing on individuals who had got awards, but did not deserve the same. I was doing the bulk of our little talk show, while Vanita was excitedly clutching onto her freshly minted certificate for securing the highest marks in mathematics in our first year in college. To be honest, I did not have a high opinion of the college awards; the paper quality was not up to the mark and the handwriting mediocre. Moreover, the awards were concentrated amongst select few individuals, creating needless suspicion in one's mind *(mine)* that the awards were rigged *(Vanita's case being an exception)*. This was not a case of sour grapes. After all, I too had bagged a certificate for 100% attendance *(never mind that I shared the award with a dozen other students)*. My rant was against the system, in general.

"Sshh Kevin. Principal Karan Patel sir is going to give away the most prestigious award of the evening," Vanita said.

A middle-aged, portly gentleman, with chalk white hair, and a perpetual smiling demeanour *(for reasons best known to him)*, took the mike and announced, "The award for the best all round student of the year goes to... Rahul Khanna!"

"*Oh no*, not again! Doesn't the fellow get bored, having to walk up to the podium, and collect a certificate each time?" It was Rahul Khanna's eleventh award of the night. He looked like the quintessential ideal student, as he strutted up to the stage to collect his award amidst a thunderous applause ringing out in the auditorium. It was apparent that Rahul Khanna knew he would win.

"Isn't he a genius?" Vanita remarked. I felt like puking.

Rahul was the poster child of an afflicted education system, which rewarded students for learning by rote. It helped that he had an excellent memory to boot. I too was a poster child of sorts, a product of the same system, but in the 'victim' category. It was not as if I didn't put in effort. In fact, my dream of replacing Rahul as the student of the year *(notwithstanding the faulty award system)* would gnaw at my sides. I devoted marathon hours seated besides my study table, and ploughing through my books. It was not about comprehension either. I believe that I had conceptual clarity on most of the subjects. But come showtime, my memory cells blanked out with sickening regularity.

During a recent oral exam in physics, the teacher asked me to enunciate Newton's most famous law. The question itself was incorrect *(Newton had many famous laws)*, but still I replied, $E = mc^2$. The teacher smiled, which is normally an encouraging sign, before asking a second question asking me to explain the dual nature of radiation and matter. I replied that they are essentially dual in nature and involved complex laws like the Photoelectric effect, which I knew but unfortunately couldn't remember. At this point, the teacher burst out laughing, which is normally *not* an encouraging sign. It was no surprise to learn later that I had flunked the test. A trip to the moon would have a higher probability of success, than bagging the student of the year award.

Later that night, after the end of the award ceremony, an ebullient Vanita dragged me to a popular eatery to celebrate. I chose a quiet corner table and plonked myself on the sole chair kept near the table. Realization dawned upon me, when Vanita who was still standing next to me, stared at me. I got up from my seat sheepishly, and offered her my seat, simultaneously pulling another chair placed near an adjoining table for myself.

"Is everything all right?"

"Yeah, everything's okay," I grumbled.

"Then please cheer up, na. Considering this is my treat, you are not allowed to get depressed at my expense."

"Yeah, yeah. But, I just don't get it. I mean, I spend hours poring over the damn books, but my results—"

"Hmmm. Don't get disheartened Kevin, this is not abnormal. Studies show that one forgets almost 40-50% of what one has read."

"Then, maybe I keep getting questions from that 40-50%."

"Don't be silly. Keep the faith, Kevin Saldanha. You have to just keep working at it. Eventually, it will all come together."

"The deluge of information we have these days, is also bogging me down. One doesn't know where to start and there is definitely no finish line. The more I read, the more I realize how little I know about the subject. "

A waiter interrupted our conversation with a menu card. "Excuse me, sir. What would you like to have?"

I took one look at the menu card contents and placed the order. "Could we have a Spinach and Ricotta Papparadelle, Pasta Ravioli, one Potato and Spinach Gnocci followed by Cannolis for dessert? Sorry Vanita, forgot to ask you, hope you are okay with Italian?"

"Wow!"

"Yes, I love Italian too."

"No, I mean that you don't seem to have any memory issues when it comes to food. You took one glance at the menu card and rattled off all those exquisite names."

"Hmmm, I never thought of it that way earlier. Now food has colour, it has character. It provides a feeling of abundance and well being. Food is the more evolved and happier version of chemistry, every dish is unique, a celebration of the interplay of the various ingredients and the skill of the chef. And this Italian food—"

"Sir, sorry to interrupt the enlightening conversation, but we regret to say that we don't have Italian food today. Our Italian chef is on leave for a week."

"You mean he has gone back to Italy?"

"No sir, he has gone to Andhra Pradesh, his native place. We are about to close, we can only serve you snacks like *missal pav, vada pav, pav bhaji, idli, dosa* and *upma*. For desert, we have vanilla ice-cream."

I looked at Vanita and sighed. Vanita hurriedly instructed the waiter to get the available snacks before I could say anything. Food was brought to us in double quick time, which raised the suspicion of whether we were being served leftovers.

After navigating through the layers of tinted oil, I took a scoop of the missal with a slice of the pav. It was unexpectedly delicious. Vanita was tearing into her dosa, when she asked me, "Have you read the Economics chapters for the day after? Prof Borde has categorically asked us to come prepared. I believe that he asks all kinds of tough questions and humiliates the students."

"To tell you the truth, I am quite stressed about Prof Borde. Economics is not my strongest subject. I am planning to read the chapters tomorrow."

"Don't end up reading comic books like you normally do, when you get stressed and waste time. By the way, could you lend me a few Tintin comic books for my cousin?"

My body stiffened instinctively. "I can, but please tell your cousin to handle these comics with great care. He should not fold any page or scribble anything on them. Each comic book has been placed in a plastic cover; your cousin should place the books back in the covers after reading. And your cousin should not lend the books to anyone else."

"Okay okay, I get the idea. I think that I will ask my cousin to buy his own set. How's your comic book collection coming along?"

"It's an ongoing process. There is a used book vendor from where I get these books at hugely discounted rates. I have asked him to inform me immediately whenever he has stocks. As a matter of fact, he has messaged me that he has got the new Superman versus Batman series. I will go and visit him tomorrow itself."

Vanita twirled the coconut chutney with her finger and said, "Please don't take offense, but if you could redistribute some of the passion and time from your comic books towards your study books, it might help."

I didn't agree, but didn't voice my onion, I mean opinion. "Would you like one more dosa to go with that coconut chutney?"

"Sorry sir, the kitchen is now closed," announced the waiter who was loitering close by, waiting impatiently for us to finish.

Needless to say, the waiter didn't get a tip when we left.

●

Ismail bookwala ran a makeshift book stall, fabricated on a portable vendor cart, close to my college. Students thronged to Ismail, to either purchase, or to dispose off used books. Ismail was resourceful; he never said no. If one wanted a book which was not available anywhere, Ismail would somehow get hold of it. And, he gave the best deal. Ismail was in this business for over two decades. I had a special equation with Ismail – he was the supplier of my comic book collection, amongst other things.

So I was perplexed when *Ismail bookwalla* stall went missing. In its place, there was a new book stall with an unfamiliar face. The stall did not have a name. A lady in her early thirties with prominent kohl-lined eyes, wearing a floral printed sari, was dusting the books. In the front of the bookstall, the lady had hung a few popular weekly magazines on a steel wire, using plastic clips. I noticed a new but ugly pillow cover hanging from one end of the wire. *What was the pillow cover doing with books?*

"Where is Ismail?" I asked the lady.

The lady stopped dusting. "Ismail? Who Ismail?"

"The book vendor who sits here regularly."

"I don't know any Ismail. Look kiddo, do you want something?"

Where has Ismail disappeared just like that? No word, no intimation. "Ah, no thank you." I turned around to go back.

"I have some fresh Superman versus Batman comic books, in case you are interested," the lady cried out behind my turned back. This caught my attention.

I turned around again to face the lady. "How much?"

"You are my first customer today. I will give you a forty percent discount."

Wow, Ismail had never given me more than 25%. I tried to push the lady, "That's too little. Make it at least 50% and it's a deal."

"Sorry kiddo. 40% is my final offer. But I can give you that beautiful pillow cover absolutely free with the books," the lady said pointing to the ugly cover at the corner.

"Huh? What will I do with the pillow cover?"

"I don't know. Normally, people sleep on it. I am sure you will put it to good use."

It was against my principles to say no to anything free, ugly or beautiful, useful or worthless. Five minutes later, I was sitting in an auto rickshaw, clutching the comic books bundled with the pillow cover.

I reached home and entered my room. There was a bed, a study table littered with books, laptop with internet connection, a cupboard to keep my stuff, a bookshelf, a trunk equipped with a lock and key containing all my valuable possessions *(namely comic books)*. Mom always complained that my room was cluttered, but I liked it the way it was; it gave me a cozy feeling. However, when I entered my room, something was not right. Everything was spick and span and in its place. The bedsheet had been changed, but the pillow cover was missing.

"Mom? Mom?" I shouted out.

My mom, who had recently celebrated her fortieth birthday, came rushing into my room.

"Ah Kevin, you are home already? Don't you like the way your room looks now? It was such a pig sty earlier. "

"Mom, I told you so many times not to touch my things. Now I have to spend so much time searching what I need."

"I don't understand. Won't it be easier to find your stuff now?"

"Never mind mom, I can't make you understand now. Accha, why is there no pillow cover on this pillow?"

"I have put the bed sheet and the pillow cover in the washing machine along with your other dirty clothes. I don't have a spare pillow cover right now, but looks like you have one? Where did you get it?"

"I, uh, a friend gave it to me."

"Why is your friend giving you such strange things? "

"Mom, I am hungry. Can I get something to eat?"

Whilst my mom went to the kitchen, I extracted my brand new Economics text book and placed it on my study table alongside my comic books. I had to decide which book to take up first. On one side were Superman and Batman, the other, Prof Borde. I made a compromise; I would first read the comic books quickly and thereafter focus wholly on Economics.

I had read the comic books thrice, before I finally willed myself to touch the Economics text book. As I tried to go through the first chapter, everything went over my head. I read every line, word by word, with the hope that my comprehension would increase, but all I achieved was frequent yawning. It was 4 p.m. I took an impromptu decision to have a quick power nap of half an hour and attack the subject, refreshed. Putting on the new pillow cover on my pillow, I lay down on the bed, placing the Economics book below the pillow. I didn't realize when I drifted off to sleep. I didn't realize it either when my mom tried to wake me up for dinner. I had slept like a log. When I did wake up, it was 8 a.m. I had slept for a record sixteen hours! *&^%$#@/&%!!*

Prof Borde was going to flay me alive in class.

●

There was pin drop silence in class as Prof Borde surveyed his potential victims like a hawk. He was a diminutive man with a ram rod posture and an elephantine ego. A man of few expressions, Prof Borde rarely handed out A in class, if ever. *That was reserved for geniuses or those with an IQ of 150+.* The average grade in his class was C.

"Okay class, let us start with a super easy question. What is normal profit?"

There were a few raised hands in class, including that of Rahul Khanna's. Mine went up involuntarily, much to my horror.

Prof Borde's eyes ignored the raised hands and rested on a girl seated on the last row, who was desperately trying to shield herself from the Prof's line of vision.

"Yes, Ms Vidya. Can you move your face to the right so that I can see you clearly? Could you explain normal profit for the benefit of the class?" Prof Borde remembered each and every name.

Vidya stood up reluctantly and spoke. "Sir, it is the average profit earned by a normal company under normal circumstances. If we were to plot the historical annual profits on normal curve, the mean of the curve would indicate normal profit."

"Let us all clap our hands for Ms Vidya for this brilliant answer." No one clapped, of course. "Ms Vidya has just tried to juxtapose statistics concepts in an economics class and treated us to some nonsensical mumbo jumbo. Sit down, Ms Vidya. Next time, please don't bother entering my class without having read your chapters. Anyone else would like to try?"

My hand went up again, the damn thing was not in my control. Prof Borde noticed it this time.

"Yes, Kevin. Would you like to enlighten all of us today?"

"Sir, if you refer to Chapter 3, page 47, para 3 in the text book, normal profit is classically defined as an economic condition occurring when the difference between a firm's total revenue and total costs both explicit and implicit, is equal to zero. Simply put, normal profit is the minimum level of profit needed for a company to remain competitive in the market. If total revenue exceeds total expenses, it is called economic profit or, alternatively, 'super-normal profit' or 'abnormal profit'. If total expenses exceed revenue, it is called economic loss. Normal profit occurs at the point at which the resources available to the firm are being efficiently used and could not be put to better use elsewhere. It is often considered the minimum amount of earnings needed in order to justify an enterprise. It is important to note that zero economic profit does not mean that the company is not earning any money. It is simply a measure of how well resources are being used relative to all possible options."

The entire class was shell shocked when I was finished. The words seemed to flow effortlessly from my mouth, it was as if I knew the answer like the back of my hand. I was in a state of bewilderment. Prof Borde's expression remained unchanged.

"I did say that this was an easy question. Okay, who would like to explain the meaning and the objectives of the Monetary Policy?"

Rahul Khanna raised his hand. My hand went up too, automatically, but Prof Borde had already zoned in on his next victim.

"Madhusudhan, would you like to explain? Madhusudhan?"

Madhusudhan stood up with a very unhappy look on his face. "Sir, I don't know the answer," he replied truthfully.

"Why is that, may I ask?"

"Monetary Policy was not part of the four chapters that you had asked us to read."

"You are talking like a baby. Are you saying that you will only read what I tell you?"

My hand was doing repeated upward thrusts. Before Prof Borde could hand over the baton to me, I stood up again and started speaking. "Sir, if I may, with your permission. If one refers to chapter 9, page 126, first para, Monetary Policy refers to the credit control measures like open market operations and change in reserve ratios adopted by the central bank of a country to achieve a) Full Employment, b) Price Stability, c) Economic Growth, d) Balance of Payments."

This time, Prof Borde exhibited a new expression that we had never seen before. His mouth was gaping wide open with astonishment. A couple of students, which included Vanita, had begun to clap, but Prof Borde's quick recovery dissuaded them from continuing. He stopped his questions abruptly and began to teach. It was like being a superhero, I felt invincible.

After the lecture, my classmates surrounded me and showered compliments. I was a star now, it was a new feeling. The only person not happy with the turn of events was Rahul Khanna. He walked off in a huff. I could see Vanita waiting patiently at one side, waiting for the crowd to disperse.

Vanita was by my side as soon as I was alone. "What happened back there?"

"Shall we go to the canteen and talk over some refreshments? I am ravenous."

The college canteen was a ramshackle structure, with paint peeling off at almost every visible square inch. Electrical wires hung from socket to socket like neglected clothes lines. The flooring was made of archaic mosaic tiles, chipped and cracked at multiple locations. Cheap plastic chairs and dysfunctional tables were placed haphazardly across the room. At the canteen counter, the harried manager was busy taking orders from the unruly students, in exchange for money and passing chits of paper to the kitchen staff behind him. I managed to shove my way across the sea of humanity and get two cups of tea along with a couple of overtly fried crisp samosas.

As we settled down on a pair of chairs which I pried from others with some difficulty, Vanita took a sip of her tea and said, "You really gave it to Prof Borde, the poor guy didn't know what hit him. It will be sometime before he recovers. So, what's going on?"

"I don't know, Vanita. I just knew. Like you said, I had to keep the faith."

"I am happy for you. Incidentally, the exam timetable has been announced. Exams are starting beginning of next month. I have a feeling that you are going to rock it this time."

Though I didn't share it with Vanita then, my instincts told me that my new power was in some way associated with my new pillow cover.

"*Yechhh...* what crap is this?" I screamed out spitting out the contents from my mouth. "Just when you think that the canteen tea couldn't get any worse, they go right ahead and prove me wrong."

"If you hate it so much, why do you keep ordering it?"

"Er, can you have my tea also?"

"Sorry Kevin, I will be barely able to finish my cup."

"Never mind, I will just have this samosa. Bloody*&^%$#@! This tastes so soggy and bland."

"Hey, I am trying to eat here, do you mind?"

Furious, I marched up to the counter manager with my half eaten samosa and glass of tea. The counter crowd had thinned.

I plonked my plate on the counter and yelled. "This is the worst samosa and tea ever, I want a refund."

The manager, a spectacled gentleman in his forties looked at me, pointed to a makeshift board below the counter table and said calmly, "Please read the sign board. It says, 'Goods once purchased will not be taken back'."

"But this food is not fit for human consumption."

"That is your opinion. The cooks have been working here for so many years. So many students have this food daily, they have no complaints. Surely you are not expecting five star food for these prices, are you?"

Knowing it was futile to argue with the hardened crook, I almost flung the plate along with its contents into the disposable plastic carton.

●

The Economics class was the tipping point in my life; the next two weeks were an upward trajectory thereon. I metamorphosed from a blink and miss personality to the prized student in every class. Every teacher worth his/ her salt wanted to interact with me. There was a lone queue from erstwhile unknown classmates to be my friend. Some even began to ask for my autograph. It seemed that the more I slept with books under my pillow, the more awesome I became.

But there was a flip side to this new found recognition and fame. Success breeds jealousy and hatred. Rahul Khanna didn't take too kindly to my success and began to spread unsavoury rumors about me. But I didn't care; I was above pettiness. It was but a matter of time before the Best Student award would come to me; I would have the last laugh.

●

Maths was the first exam of the series. I had kept four books and one note book under my pillow. It was a little uncomfortable but I managed to fall asleep eventually.

As anticipated, the exam was a roaring success. It was by far, the easiest paper of my life. Not only had I finished the paper half an hour before time, I had written two answers for each question. This may be a little difficult to imagine for a quantitative paper like Maths wherein there is only one right answer, but then, I was inspired.

After the end of the exam, I rushed to meet Vanita.

"Fantastic paper, eh? I am sure you are going to get the top marks again."

"Speak for yourself, pal. Look around you."

It was a strange sight. Gloom and despair were the predominant moods, majority of the students were sulking, a few were even crying.

"This was the toughest Maths paper in the last decade. Half the class is expected to fail. I am myself hoping to pass by the skin of my teeth."

"You don't say?"

"Looks like you have really cracked the code, eh?"

"Shall we go out to celebrate?"

"Look, I am not really in the mood."

"But I am. And considering it's my treat, you are not allowed to get depressed at my expense."

"Haha. Very funny. Okay. Which place?"

"The Italian joint which serves missal pav and dosa?"

●

"What would you like to have, sir?" It was our old waiter friend again.

"There you go again. Is your Italian chef back?"

"No sir, he left the job. But now we can offer you Japanese *sushi*. Here, please have a look at our menu card."

"Where is your Japanese chef from?"

"Haryana."

"Okay. We will have tuna sashimi, teriyaki shitake and spicy aubergine with some wasabi please."

Once the waiter had left, Vanita reminded me to reveal my secret.

"Do you do take any medication or are you doing some special brain exercises or what?"

"Naah, nothing so complicated. All I do is sleep, and voila!"

"Are you trying to pull a fast one on me?"

"I am serious." I stood up, bent forward and whispered in Vanita's ear. "The secret is in my pillow cover. I just keep a book under it and sleep over it. As simple as that."

"I don't believe it. This is insane."

"I know it is difficult to believe, but you have seen the results. Would you like to try it out? But you will need to come home."

"*Oooh!* That's so exciting."

Food was served in twenty minutes, which implied lesser possibility of leftovers this time around.

"That looks great. Thanks again, Kevin."

"My pleasure. You must try the sushi with some wasabi, but not too much. Let me show you."

I took a sashimi and dipped it gently into the wasabi, before popping it into my mouth.

"How's it?"

"That's funny. Let me try again." I dipped another sashimi piece and dabbed it with generous doses of wasabi this time, before putting it into my mouth.

"What's wrong?"

"This thing tastes like cardboard. And the wasabi tastes like clay. Waiter? Waiter?"

The waiter came running. "Yes sir, what seems to be the problem?"

"How can you guys even call this sushi? This is really pathetic food. Japanese chef from Haryana. Ha!"

"Sir, Rampal has worked in the house a few Japanese families, he comes with multiple recommendations. We have never had complaints so far."

"So, I am lying, eh? Call your chef, Rampal."

Rampal came running from the kitchen. A tall, lanky male, Rampal had donned a white coloured chef's hat. He dipped a sashimi piece into the wasabi, breathed a sigh of relief and remarked, "Personally, I don't like sushi. But this tastes yummy, sir."

"Wait. Vanita, you try it and tell them."

Vanita took a small sample of all the dishes. I waited impatiently for her to announce the verdict. *There was no way I was paying for this horsecrap.* Vanita looked at the waiter and the chef and instructed both of them. "Can you give us five minutes alone, please?"

"Sure ma'am."

Once the waiter and the chef were out of earshot, Vanita looked and me and remarked, "What is wrong with you, Kevin? This is fine authentic sushi."

This was all terribly confusing. So I went to the washroom, gargled a few times, came back to my seat, took an entire spoon of wasabi and proceeded to put it into my mouth.

"Don't!" Vanita cried out. It was too late.

I shook my head sideways. "Still tastes like clay."

"But how is this possible? Wait, there is one possible explanation," Vanita banged the table with her fist.

"Easy there, this table is not exactly sturdy."

"I get it now. When you gained a power, you also lost something."

"What do you mean?"

"Don't you get it? You sacrifice something to get something, that's the law of nature. You are losing your sense of taste. It's the price you paid for your new-found academic brilliance."

"Huh? That's a wild hypothesis. If it were true, then how come I didn't have taste issues since the last two weeks?"

"Is it? Can you try to remember how did your food taste since the last two weeks?"

"That's not difficult. I have been having only home food. There were a few occasions when mom had forgotten to add salt and spices but—"

"Is it normal for your mom to forget?"

"Uhh… no, she makes it a habit of personally validating the taste before serving the food."

"Bingo. Then there was the college canteen episode."

"You are suggesting that I made a mistake? You are not trying to defend that horrid canteen food, are you?"

"No, what I am suggesting is that your sense of taste would have been flickering on and off, until it finally gave away today."

●

I was devastated and went into denial mode initially. But subsequent trials with extreme substances like *chilly* powder and *karela* confirmed Vanita's hypothesis – they were all tasteless. To add to my misery, the trials created havoc with my bowel movements. I had to make frequent visits to the loo.

Vanita ate to her heart's content, while I watched with a tinge of jealousy and regret. I began to wonder at the prospect of more side effects with the passage of time. The thought made me shudder. Was the process irreversible? But then, did I want to reverse the process at all? I couldn't bear the thought of Rahul Khanna bagging another student of the year award at my expense. Besides, the exams were still underway, I had not studied one iota. *Naah, it was all worth it. I had gone from being a nobody to a somebody in class. First the student of the year award, after that, jo hoga dekha jayega.*

I returned home and searched for my Biology textbook. We had Biology exam the next morning and I was keen to maximize on my sleep. As I prepared to lie down and put the text book below the pillow, I noticed to my horror that the pillow cover was missing.

"Mom, Mom? Can you turn down the volume of that stupid serial that you are watching? Mom?" I shouted out.

Mom lowered the volume and shouted back. " Why are you shouting, Kevin?"

"Where is my pillow cover?"

"The ugly one? I washed it. "

"Washed it? What do you mean by washed it? I barely even used it. I don't understand why you have to touch my things without asking me. I have told you so many times, but you never listen. Mom? Mom?"

"Jeez, why are you getting so upset? Use the clean one," my mom replied nonchalantly before increasing the volume of the TV again.

I frantically searched for the pillow cover amongst the pile of washed clothes, finally tracing it on the clothes line. It was still wet. I grabbed it and immediately began to iron it. My effort bore fruit. After ten minutes, the pillow cover was dry and ready for use. Heaving a sigh of relief, I put the cover on the naked pillow, placed the Biology textbook below the pillow, lay down and closed my eyes. My heart was beating rapidly with all the built up stress, I tossed and turned in bed. It would a while before I would finally drop off to sleep.

•

Something was terribly wrong. I was sweating profusely and an invisible hammer was repeatedly pounding my head in short, rhythmic intervals. In addition, my body felt itchy at various places. Barely five minutes were left for the bell to ring and end my misery. In the last couple of hours, I had been able to write down my name, roll number and class in the Biology exam answer paper. The questions didn't make any sense to me, they might as well have been written in another language. This would be the toughest Biology paper in decades. I was pretty sure that we would achieve a new benchmark as a class, a hundred percent failure rate.

The bell rang. *Finally!*

I ran out of the examination hall, Vanita was already waiting for me outside.

"That was one hell of a paper. These examiners are so unpredictable, what were they trying to prove? Hey, what's with that silly grin?"

"That was the easiest paper ever!"

It was as if someone had knocked the wind out of me. "*Easy? Easy?* From which god damn angle was it *easy?*"

"Every single question. I am sure that I am going to hit bull's eye. But why am I even bragging to you? You would have hit the ball out of the park, I'm sure."

Did the book slip out of place? Or had I placed the wrong text book under my pillow?

"You look disturbed, is everything okay?"

"I – I – am finding it difficult to breathe. I need to get out of here."

As I hurried away with Vanita in tow, I couldn't help but notice a festive spirit in the air. Joyous students were giving each other the high fives as if each one had won a million dollar lottery. *Idiots! They made me sick.*

●

Disturbing thoughts proliferated in my mind. I needed answers. *Desperately.*

I was breathless from all the running, when I reached the used book vendor's location. Ismail bookwala was back.

"Hello Kevin, so nice to see you again. Do you want any comics? I have the complete set of Asterix originals, in mint condition."

"Ismail, where is that lady?"

Ismail wrinkled his eyebrows. "What lady?"

"Arrey, that lady who sold used books when you were not here."

"When I was not here? But I was always here. I have been here for the last twenty years. Why will I go anywhere?"

"The lady with the floral printed sari and kohl in her eyes, Ismail. She even gave me some comics at 40% discount."

"40% discount? Hahaha, nice once. I think you have been studying too hard, Kevin. You need a break. Take these Asterix comics. I will give you our usual special discount: 25%."

Was Ismail lying? Or was my mind playing tricks on me?

●

"Kevin Saldanha," announced the Starbucks waiter as he held out a tray of iced caramel macchiato and a classic hot chocolate. I took the tray and placed it on our table, handing the glass of classic hot chocolate to Vanita.

Looking out of the glass window next to our table, I sighed and remarked, "My head is all messed up right now. Don't know what's real or unreal anymore. But one thing is for sure. Bye bye Student of the year."

"Aww, don't feel bad. It was good while it lasted. But you have learnt a valuable lesson. There is no short cut to hard work and sacrifice."

"Yeah, yeah, spare me the bull! Hey, did you just see that woman on the other side of the road?"

"Which woman?"

"The one with the sari."

"There are so many women on the road wearing a sari."

"Arrey, she is the one that gave me the pillow cover."

At that very moment, the mysterious lady looked in my direction; she seemed to have recognized me. I rushed out of Starbucks, with a confused Vanita behind me.

"Where is she? "

I looked all around, straining my eyes. Surprise, surprise, the lady was now manning an apple cart! Her signature kohl eye lining looked as prominent as ever.

I confronted the lady. "I had been searching for you. Where had you disappeared" ?

"Hello, kid. I am always available for those who need me. Can I offer you some apples?"

"What happened to your used books stall?"

"Used books? Oh that! I closed that shop a long time ago."

"Do you remember giving me a pillow cover? It is useless now."

"You mean it is torn? I can't help you. You need to visit a tailor."

"No, no, you don't understand. The pillow cover had some kind of power to increase memory instantly. That power is gone now. In addition, I have lost my sense of taste."

"You have an active imagination, kid. I gave you the pillow cover without any charge; it was your choice to take it. Hence there is no question of a refund. But I can make you another offer. If you buy two dozen apples from me, I can give you this shiny green ceramic mug absolutely free. I have only one piece left."

I looked at the mug closely. It was a hideous looking specimen. The green colour was patchy and chipped at a number of locations. The drinking edge was not entirely smooth, had a few unfinished protrusions. The mug handle was more of a broken handle bar than a smooth arc. *This mug did not even deserve to be given free of cost.*

"What does this mug do?"

"You can use it drink water, tea, coffee, milk, soft drinks, etc. You can also use it as a show piece in your house or a place to keep your toothbrushes and tooth paste—"

"Yes, yes... but what else? Is there anything special about it?"

"Yes, it is made from special bone china. Look, it is even printed below the cup – Special bone china, made in China."

"No, no. I mean, is there anything magical about it?"

The lady scratched her head and said, "I can't understand what you are saying. What do you really want, kid? Are you interested in buying some apples or not?"

I thought hard for a minute and sighed. *What if—*

"Ok, how much?"

"Two hundred rupees for two kgs of apples. Mug is free, of course."

"I am asking about the mug. You can keep the stupid apples. They are all green anyway."

"Sorry kid, it is against my principles. And if you want to pay, you will need to take the apples."

Five minutes later, I had rejoined Vanita inside Starbucks. She subjected me to a barrage of questions. "What did that lady tell you? What's with all those green apples? And where did you get that dreadful mug?"

Dejected, tired and confused, I dismissed Vanita's volley with a wave of my hand. Placing the apples and the mug on the table, I took a much needed sip of my coffee. The warm fluid rejuvenated me instantly.

"This caramel macchiato is fantastic! I love the way the flavour Kenyan Arabica beans have been roasted and extracted. There is a fresh blooded juiciness with a tell tale grapefruit flavour."

An amused Vanita looked at me closely and then asked the Starbucks attendant behind the counter, "Which coffee beans have you used in the macchiato?"

"We ran out of Indian coffee beans, so we used premium Kenyan whole beans. Hope you liked them, ma'am?"

Vanita looked at me at amazement and exclaimed, "Wow. How on earth did you know all that by just taking a sip? I didn't know that you were a coffee aficionado."

It was my turn to be puzzled. "I am *not*. I have no clue how that happened. "

Vanita smiled and remarked, "Welcome back."

It was the mug! I was both relieved and delighted as I looked at the mug fondly. As I took a second sip of my macchiato, I closed my eyes and experienced the bliss.

When I opened my eyes again, I noticed that Vanita's expression had changed, she was looking concerned.

"You know, I was thinking—"

The thought struck me even before Vanita could express it. *I had not even used the damn mug. So how did I get my new super taste buds? And what had I lost out this time round?* Fear of the uncertain gripped my heart as I turned and looked out of the Starbucks glass window.

The mysterious lady with the kohl lined eyes had disappeared into thin air.

Gubbara Yadav's adventure

Gubbara Yadav

That's it! I have decided to go on strike. My thankless and heartless employer, Lilliput Yadav, has exploited me for far too long. I have worked like a donkey at his farm for the last four years. My employer has prospered but what have I got in return? Only abuses and insults, never any appreciation. My youth and good looks are all but gone. The living conditions are abysmal; my accommodation is a ramshackle, crumbling cottage with gaping holes of various hues in the roof (great for day lighting and ventilation, but a trifle inconvenient during the rains, when it gets flooded). Not to mention the odd snake that invariably finds its way in. But does the employer care? No sir. The food is fit for cows; bland, tasteless and repetitive. I am sure that the grass is greener elsewhere.

If that were not enough, my employer insists on calling me Gubbara Yadav. A moniker given by his infernal youngest son Twinkle Yadav, the lousy name has stuck. One should not be fooled by Twinkle Yadav's angelic face; he is the devil incarnate. Twinkle has an unhealthy interest in me, I am his primary source of amusement; be it mixing chilies in my food, bursting firecrackers when I am sleeping, guiding a few snakes into my accommodation or jumping onto my back at any given moment.

●

Lilliput Yadav

I have decided to sell off Gubbara. All this while, we have treated him like a member of the family and showered our affection on him.We have provided him shelter, given him the best quality food, taken care of him when he is sick.What did I expect in return? A little help in the fields, from time to time? But no sir. He has to do the opposite of what I say. If I say go west, he goes east. If I say go north, he goes south. Sometimes, I think he does that on purpose. All he wants to do is sit in the house, hog and become fatter by the day.

If that were not enough, if he sees his reflection anywhere, he has to stop and admire himself. This is not normal behaviour.What he should realize is that he has a tail, a big nose and two huge horns, like any other bull.

I thought that if he does not like to work in the fields, the very least he could do is breed. I even placed two beautiful, healthy cows in his barn, with the hope that something will happen. But the fellow just sits in a corner, munching on his hay. Sometimes I wonder if he is gay? Total disappointment!

All our pampering has gone to his head. But no more. There is a mega town fair coming up next fortnight; it is an ideal opportunity for me. All that fat he has put on at my expense should finally fetch me a good price.

Gubbara Yadav

I almost forgot to add, my employer has forced me to share my already crappy accommodation with two of the ugliest cows that I have ever seen. All they do is look at me and keep mooing at each other. And these are the long irritating moos. They sit on their behinds and do nothing the whole day. Just because they give a little milk here and there, Lilliput Yadav treats them like queens. I could have done the same, if I had udders.

For the record, I am not gay. Although, I can't say the same for sure about the two cows.

●

Lilliput Yadav

I am feeling lucky today, I can feel it in my bones. So many visitors at the cattle stalls and with so much money to spend. This is one amazing fair! I am going to make a killing today by selling off Gubbara!

Gubbara Yadav

I am feeling lucky today, I can feel it in my bones. A new home, a new employer and a new job. Anything and anyone will be better than Lilliput and company.

So many visitors in this fair today, I am sure that I will be in huge demand.

Bye bye Lilliput. Bye bye Twinkle. Bye Bye ugly cows.

Lilliput Yadav

What a lousy fair! I have been standing here under the sun for such a long time and not a single visitor to my stall. Nobody seems to be interested in El Fatso here. Just my luck!

Wait, that guy seems to be taking a keen interest in Gubbara. Doesn't look like an Indian. Is he a foreigner? He must be an American, should have lots of dollars. I have to sell Gubbara to him somehow or the other.

Hey, he is moving away. I have to stop him!

I ran behind the foreigner and yelled out. "Stop, stop! Why are you leaving, *gora*?"

The foreigner turned around, surprised. "Excuse me?"

"*Atithi Devo Bhava,* sir. *Atithi Devo Bhava.*" I replied hurriedly.

"*Huh?* I don't understand, mate."

"Are you American, sir? I love America, great country."

"Good for *ya*, mate. But I am not from America."

My face fell, but only for a brief moment. "*Aah*, then which country, sir?"

"I am from Australia, mate."

"Australia? That must be near America, *no*? Both start with A and end with A."

"*Fair dinkum!* They are only about 10, 000 miles apart. Now, if ya will excuse me, I have work to do. See ya later."

"It was nice to meet you. Have a great day, sir. Please say hi to the other Australians for me." The fellow had already begun to walk away.

Gubbara Yadav

What is he doing? Has Lilliput lost his marbles? I cannot allow my only chance to go abroad, slip through my hooves. Something has to be done, quick.

Lilliput Yadav

All of a sudden, Gubbara began to bellow loudly. I realized my folly as I ran behind the Australian again and tapped him on his back. He looked a trifle annoyed.

"*Crikey!* What now, mate?"

"I saw that you were looking at my bull with a lot of interest. You want to buy? I will give you a very good price."

"That's a lot of bull *ya* got there, mate. Too fat."

Gubbara Yadav

Whom is he calling fat, eh? This fellow needs glasses. I may be healthy, but definitely not fat.

I bellowed my resentment.

Lilliput Yadav

"Don't judge him by his looks, sir. He is a prized breed, just like the Sumo wrestlers. Would you call Sumo wrestlers fat? No, na? We have fed him a special diet of only butter, roti and cake since birth."

"What's his specialty?"

"Yes sir, he is very special."

"No mate, I meant what is he good for? Is he any good at bull fighting? Is he any good at breeding?"

"Sir, we are essentially non-violent people. So we have not exposed him to any kind of fighting. But he would be very good at breeding."

"*Would*? Has he not bred yet?"

"*Uh-huh*, he is very shy. I am confident that once you expose him to a variety of cows, he will work his magic."

The Australian smiled at me and shook his head. "Sorry, mate."

"Okay, I will give you a very special price, only for you – Rs 45, 000."

The grin on the Australian's face widened.

"No? Okay, Rs 40, 000 fixed price. Best deal you will get in the entire market."

The Australian continued smiling and didn't utter a word.

"Oh come on! Okay Rs 35, 000 full and final price. I am already making a huge loss. Sir, please say yes now. Please?"

The Australian looked at me in the eye and said pointedly, "I will give *ya* Rs 15, 000. A darned good offer for this bucket of lard. Take it or leave it."

"Sir, how can you bargain like this? This bull is not an animal; he is almost like a member of our family. You can't devalue a member of your family. Rs 16, 000, not a rupee less."

The Australian extended his right hand gleefully and shook my hand. "A deal, mate."

It is a huge loss, financially speaking, but I am glad that I finally managed to get rid of the dead wood. Now Gubbara is someone else's problem.

Gubbara Yadav

Such a low price? This is so humiliating!

Money exchanged hands; I had a new employer at last! The foreigner led me away gently and goaded me to board a large open truck with the help of a makeshift ramp. The truck was already loaded with assorted cows, bulls, buffaloes and a solitary pig. There was barely any place to stand. I couldn't help noticing that everyone had formed groups and was busy chatting away. The pig was the exception, the odd one out. Standing in a corner all by himself, he was looking miserable. I couldn't help feeling sorry for him. Making my way through the crowd, I joined the pig and tried to strike up a conversation.

"All alone, eh?"

The pig looked at me, devoid of expression. "Yes, I was a given away as part of a package deal."

I didn't understand, but tried to empathize with his situation. "Oh!"

"So, are you excited about going abroad?"

The pig looked at me for a long time, face still expressionless. "Who told you that we are going abroad?"

"Nobody told me. But you know that our employer is Australian, right? So it is logical—"

"And you think that we are going to Australia in this truck?"

"Er, yes. Why? Is something wrong?"

"Hahaha," the pig laughed, face again expressionless. "You are a strange fellow. My dear fellow, I have news for you. They are taking us to the abattoir."

"Abattoir? Is that some kind of a tourist place?"

"Not exactly. It's a slaughter house," said the pig, matter of factly.

My feelings of euphoria were instantly replaced by those of dread and horror. "Wow! You are trying to pull my legs, aren't you?"

The pig shook his head gravely.

"But how is that possible? That foreigner seemed so friendly and kind hearted; surely he wouldn't do this to us? Besides, isn't killing cattle illegal in India now?"

"Not if the abattoir is licensed. There, we will be sorted into various categories and executed by CO_2 gassing. Once we conk off, we will be eviscerated, cut up into pieces, refrigerated, packed and sold off."

"That's brutal and grotesque! How do you know so much?"

"A pig is amongst the top ten smartest animals in the hierarchy of the animal kingdom. We can give the chimpanzees a run for their money. Unfortunately, we have never got our due, because of our looks."

"Okay, but I don't want to die. Please save me."

"Why do you want to live in this cruel world ruled by human beings? We will all die some day, better now than later. The faster we get out of the cycle of karma and rebirth, the better for us."

Just my luck to encounter a spiritual pig.

"I have no clue what you are saying. But can you at least try to help me escape?"

"Even if I help you, where will you go? Remember, our owners have sold us out. My case is *toh* even worse; I have been given away free, just like that. We are the discards of society; our value is not in our life but in our death."

Please spare me the morose lecture. This guy is suffering from a serious depression.

"Will you help me escape or not?"

"Hmmm. All right, if that is what you want, dear bull. We are lucky that the truck has not yet started moving. I will create a simple diversion and you can use the opportunity to make your escape."

"What about you, dear pig?"

"I think that I will stay and leave my fate to destiny."

Without warning, the pig threw himself to the floor and began to flail his legs. "Oink, Oink, Oink, Oink," he bleated loudly. Other cattle made space for the pig immediately, out of fear.

"Oink, Oink, Oink, Oink."

The pig's actions became increasingly animated; it was as if he was having childbirth spasms. The onboard action attracted the attention of the cattle supervisor (an Indian) and the Australian, who were standing nearby.

"*Oi!* What's all that racket, mate?"

The cattle supervisor entered the truck and saw the pig rolling from side to side. He observed him for a minute or so and then remarked, "Something is wrong with the pig, sir. This is the problem of getting something free; you can never trust the quality."

Intrigued, the Australian boarded the truck too. He looked at the pig intently, who seemed to be giving an Oscar award winning performance. Other cattle had surrounded the scene of the spectacle; they were looking on with keen interest. The truck ramp had been left unguarded. Making my way quietly to the rear of the truck, I tiptoed gingerly down the ramp praying that no one would see me. No sooner had I touched the ground, than I ran for dear life. I ran like a gazelle splicing through the wind, against the backdrop of the evening sun. *(Okay, that may have been a slight exaggeration).*

Men, children and women made way for me, screaming, "Look out, mad bull, mad bull!"

I ran and ran until I could run no more. Panting and out of breath, I stopped under a huge tree, near the road side. My entire body was aching. When my eyes fell upon a spread of luscious green grass sprawled across the vast countryside, I realized how hungry and thirsty I was. I began to graze with a vengeance. It was the yummiest food I had tasted in months! I grazed to my heart's content and then sat down contentedly. Chewing the cud in the mouth slowly, I began to ponder over what the pig had told me. *Where should I go now?* Belly full, my eye lids began to droop.

"Oink, Oink."

My tail tried to swat away the unwarranted disturbance. It was an automatic, sub conscious, reflex action.

"Oink, Oink."

I opened my eyes partially and saw the familiar silhouette of the pig standing next to me.

"Are we both dead? "

"No, we are both pretty much alive." It was the pig all right, his face as expressionless as ever.

My eyes opened wide. "So nice to see you again, dear pig. How did you escape?"

"I didn't escape, I was thrown out. They suspected me of having some kind of contagious disease."

"That's great news. But how did you find me?"

"A pig is amongst the top ten smartest animals in the hierarchy of the animal kingdom. We can give the chimpanzees a run for their money. Unfortunately, we have never got our due, because of our looks."

"Yes, yes, you have already told me all that before."

"So what will you do now?"

"I don't know; I'm quite confused. Should I remain in the wild or should I go to knock at some stranger's door? I don't want to go back to Lilliput."

"Hmmm. In option number one, much as you like your freedom, you are essentially a domesticated creature. This means that you cannot survive on your own in the wild. Strike out the first option. In option two, if you go to a stranger's house, then either you will get thrown out or you may be taken in. In case you are taken in, you could be ill treated and sold off again or you could get lucky and get a good master. But that is a very remote possibility akin to an alien landing on the earth. Let us come to the third option – going back to your existing master."

"*Noo*—I don't want to go back. Besides, what is the guarantee that he won't sell me off again?"

"There is no guarantee, but he is a known devil. If you make yourself valuable to him, why should he get rid of you? To be honest, looking at you, a little bit of field work would do you no harm."

"But I have to share my lousy accommodation with two ugly cows."

"So what? There are so many creatures that never get a single option in their lives and here you are cribbing with not one but two options. Many bulls would kill to be in your position. It takes time, but if you adjust yourself mentally, you will be able to accept their presence. Procreation is a natural process of life and you should not shy away from your job responsibilities. Make yourself indispensable to your employer, that's the mantra for survival."

I sighed, much of what the pig said didn't make any sense to me. But I kind of got the gist. "I guess you are right. Much as I hate myself for it, I will go back to Lilliput Yadav and company. But there is a problem;I don't know the way."

"Do you know where he stays?"

"Yes, in Sitamarhi village."

"That's easy, then. Take this straight road and keep going until you come to a huge banana plantation. Then take the road to the right and continue to go straight. You will reach your village."

The pig never ceased to amaze me. "How do you know all this?"

"A pig is amongst the top ten smartest animals in the hierarchy of the animal kingdom. We can give the chimpanzees a run for their money. Unfortunately, we—"

I put up a leg to interrupt. "Yes, yes. I know, I know. Say, why don't you come with me? It will be great fun."

"No, dear bull. I have to find my own path."

"Are you sure?"

"Yes, absolutely sure. I am searching for inner peace and someday I hope to find it."

"You are queer, dear pig. I have no idea what you are saying but it has been a pleasure knowing you. Take care. Hope we meet again someday."

"Of course, if that is what destiny has written for us. Good luck and good bye."

I followed the instructions given by the pig and reached the village safely, without any further incident. There were only two people in the house, Mrs Yadav and Twinkle Yadav. Mouth agape, Mrs Yadav dropped her aluminum utensil. It was as if she had seen a ghost.

Twinkle Yadav leapt with joy on seeing me. Embracing me, he gave out shouts of joy. Had I been a human, my eyes would have become moist with emotion. Instead, I looked at Twinkle solemnly. It was apparent that Twinkle Yadav had missed me so sorely. *I had completely misjudged the little angel; he has a heart of gold.*

Where is Lilliput Yadav? Aah, there he comes!

Lilliput Yadav

Who is that bull in my house? He looks so much like Gubbara. Wait a minute, wait a minute, what the—— He IS Gubbara! How on earth did he find my house and come back? Has he escaped or has the Australian let him go?

I must take him back to the Australian. Hold it right there, Lilliput! Have you lost it completely? Gubbara has returned on his own; you have not stolen him. It's god's wish. Do you want to anger god by going against his wish? I thought so! Finders keepers, losers weepers.

And don't even think about returning the money to that Australian. He didn't think twice before giving you such a low price for Gubbara. God served him right, justice has been done. The money is yours; you got it fair and square.

Twinkle Yadav

Thank you dear god for returning Gubbara to me. I missed him so much! Life was so boring and dreary without him. I could not try out my pranks with those two silly cows for fear of my father beating me up.

Now that Gubbara is back, we will have lots of fun together again. But I can't trust father anymore, so I am going to have to put Gubbara in shackles. It's for his own good. Let him get some rest tonight; we will have a busy day tomorrow. I am going to tie some fire crackers to his tail and we will see as to how fast he can run; I hope he will not disappoint me. In the evening, I will organize a hoop throwing competition wherein I will challenge people to throw hoops around his horns and charge them money for it. We are partners now; I will keep the money and give the hoops to Gubbara.

LOVED IT? LIKED IT? HATED IT?

Post your review
On

amazon

goodreads

Thank you